Nobody can write Forbidden Fantasies like Cara Summers...

Led into Temptation

"Sensationally sensual...this tale of a forbidden, guilt-ridden love is a delight. Brimming with diverse, compelling characters, scorching hot love scenes, romance and even a ghost, this story is unforgettable."
—*Romancejunkies.com*

"This deliciously naughty fantasy takes its time heating up, but it's worth the wait! 4 ½ stars."
—*RT Book Reviews*

Taken Beyond Temptation

"Great characters with explosive chemistry, a fun intrigue-flavored plot and a high degree of sensuality add up to an excellent read! 4 ½ stars."
—*RT Book Reviews*

"Filled with intrigue, mystery, humor, sizzling hot love scenes...a well-matched couple, a surprise ending and a ghost, this story is unforgettable and definitely a winner."
—*Romancejunkies.com*

Twice the Temptation

"Well written! Fans will be delighted to see their favorites return for brief appearances. 4 stars."
—*RT Book Reviews*

"Cara Summers has penned two tales in *Twice the Temptation* which will not be forgotten, but will live on in the reader's fantasies."
—*Cataromance.com*

Dear Reader,

I want to thank all of you for waiting so patiently for the third and final book of my Forbidden Fantasies trilogy, *No Desire Denied*.

Seven years ago, spurred on by their father's wedding, a bottle of champagne and a serious case of lust for their new stepmom's gorgeous sons, Adair, Piper and Nell MacPherson each wrote down their most secret sexual fantasies about one of the Sutherland men and buried their admissions in a stone arch on their family's estate. Then they promptly forgot about them. Almost.

One by one, the Sutherland triplets—first Cam, then Duncan and now finally Reid—have been drawn back to Castle MacPherson, not only by the legendary power of the stones and the erotic fantasies penned all those years ago, but also to right a wrong and restore a stolen bride's long-missing dowry to its rightful owners.

I hope you enjoy Reid and Nell's story as much as I enjoyed writing it. For more information on the Sutherland triplets and the earlier books in the series, *No Risk Refused* and *No Holds Barred,* visit my website, www.carasummers.com.

May all your forbidden fantasies come true!

Cara Summers

No Desire Denied

—

Cara Summers

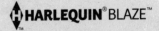

Recycling programs
for this product may
not exist in your area.

ISBN-13: 978-0-373-79776-9

NO DESIRE DENIED

Copyright © 2013 by Carolyn Hanlon

Printed in U.S.A.

ABOUT THE AUTHOR

Was Cara Summers born with the dream of becoming a published romance novelist? No. But now that she is, she still feels her dream has come true. And she owes it all to her mother, who handed her a Harlequin romance novel years ago and said, "Try it. You'll love it." Mom was right! Cara has written over forty stories for the Blaze and Temptation lines, and she has won numerous awards, including a Lifetime Achievement Award for Series Storyteller of the Year from *RT Book Reviews*. When she isn't working on new books, she teaches in the writing program at Syracuse University.

Books by Cara Summers

HARLEQUIN BLAZE

To get the inside scoop on Harlequin Blaze and its talented writers, be sure to check out blazeauthors.com.

Other titles by this author available in ebook format.

To my three sons, Kevin, Brian and Brendan. As you have grown into fine young men, I have watched you cherish and protect the ones you love. You have inspired my heroes for over forty books. My wish is that you continue to care for each other and for your families, and I know that it will come true.

To the best editor in the world, Brenda Chin. Thanks for everything, especially your unwavering belief in me.

To Dr. Tucker Harris. Thanks for everything.

Prologue

Glen Loch, New York, summer 1812

ELEANOR CAMPBELL MACPHERSON sat in the gazebo that her late husband, Angus, had built for her and frowned at the sketch on her easel. This had always been her favorite place on the castle grounds to draw and to think. But today neither was going well. The story she was telling in the picture wasn't completed and neither was her mission.

Since his death a year ago, Angus had been visiting her in dreams and sending her visions that were helping her to right an old wrong. But for the last two months, the dreams hadn't been so clear. And she was anxious to finish. Wasn't she?

Or was she afraid that, once she buried the last of the Stuart sapphires, Angus would be lost to her forever?

When the pain around her heart tightened at the thought, she set down her pencils and walked over to sit on the stone steps that led into the garden. She missed him so much, and there wasn't anyplace on the castle grounds she could go that didn't bring back memories.

The gazebo had originally been her idea. She and Angus had chosen the spot for it together, because it offered views of the lake, as well as the castle and the stone arch, both of which he'd built to fulfill his promises to her. Of course, Angus, impulsive as always, had designed the gazebo and started construction immediately. He'd used stones for the foundation and chosen the sturdiest of woods for the benches, the railing and the roof. It had been his gift to her on their first anniversary.

Looking out on everything that Angus had built for her and everything that they'd created together, she recalled that long-ago day when the castle had still been under construction and the gardens had been in their infancy. It was their anniversary, and they'd placed the last stones in the arch together, stones that Angus had brought with him to the New World when he'd stolen her away from her home in Scotland.

He'd built the arch in a clearing at the far end of the gardens, just before the land sloped sharply upward into the mountains. It was almost an exact replica of the stone arch that had stood for hundreds of years in the gardens of the Campbell estate in Scotland. According to the legend that her mother and two older sisters had told her, the stone arch had the power from ancient times to unite true lovers. All you had to do was kiss your lover beneath the arch, and that was it. A *happy ever after* was guaranteed.

Well, she'd certainly kissed Angus many times beneath it. And she'd never forget the night she'd met him there for the last time. Having been promised to another man, she'd snuck out of the ball celebrating the engagement. She had been wearing her fiancé's gift to her—a sapphire necklace and earring set that had been bequeathed to his family for service to the Scottish court. Mary Stuart had worn the jewels at her coronation, and Eleanor's husband-to-be had insisted that she wear them at the ball as a display of his love for her.

With a smile, Eleanor recalled how fast her heart had been beating when she'd raced through the gardens to say a final goodbye to Angus. There could be no future for them, because she had to honor the arrangement her parents had made. Plus Angus's family and hers had been blood enemies for years. But before she could say a word, Angus had kissed her.

Even when she'd tried to say no, he hadn't listened. Impatient, impetuous and irresistible, Angus had simply swept her away.

Exactly what she'd wanted him to do.

Just the memory had her heart beating fast again.

That had only been the beginning of their story. Eleanor swept her gaze from the stone arch over the lush gardens to the castle and then back again. Angus had delivered on all of his promises. Her husband and lover of fifty years believed in building things that lasted—a marriage, a home, a family. Because of Angus's story-spinning talent, the legendary power of the replicated stone arch had taken root and spread. Their own three sons had married beneath the stones. Angus invited anyone to tap into the power of the legend, and many Glen Loch locals had taken advantage of his generosity.

Leaning back against a pillar, Eleanor closed her eyes, and let the scent of the flowers and hum of the insects help her find the inner peace the garden always brought her. She'd never once regretted her decision to leave everything behind in Scotland and come here to New York with Angus. In fact, it was the best decision she'd ever made. She had only one regret—on the night she'd run away with Angus, she'd taken the Stuart sapphires with her.

With her eyes still closed, she slipped a hand into her pocket and closed her fingers around the soft leather pouch that held the sapphire necklace that Mary Stuart wore at her coronation. Everything had happened so fast that long-ago night; once Angus had kissed her, she'd forgotten all about the sapphires. Only when it was too late had her conscience begun to trouble her. Any attempt to contact her family or return the jewels would have increased the chances that she and Angus would be found.

Her sons and her daughters-in-law believed the jewels had been her dowry, no doubt because she'd worn them in the formal portrait that hung in the main parlor of the castle. But they hadn't been her dowry. A man who'd loved her had given her the jewels, and she'd betrayed both his love and his trust. That made her worse than a thief.

Angus had always known about her troubled conscience, and he'd promised on his deathbed that he would help her right the old wrong. That was why he was visiting her now. The initial visions he'd sent to her had been so clear. In one, she'd seen a young woman with reddish-gold curls discovering a single earring in the stone arch. Eleanor had taken it as a sign to hide the first earring there. In the dreams that had followed, she'd seen a woman with long dark hair finding an earring in the old caves in the cliff face. So that's where Eleanor had hidden the second one.

But in her latest dreams, all she could see for sure were the blue stones of the necklace glowing so brightly that the features and surroundings of the young woman holding them were blurred. All Eleanor knew was that she had long blond hair, and she looked vaguely familiar.

A gull cried out over the lake, and squirrels chattered in nearby trees. Ignoring both, Eleanor kept her eyes closed and focused on bringing the girl's image into her mind again. This time it wasn't so blurry. She suddenly realized why the young woman had looked so familiar. She looked similar to how Eleanor herself had looked when she'd had that portrait painted.

As recognition slipped into her mind, she heard Angus's voice.

Her name is Nell, and like her sisters, she believes in the legendary power of the stones enough to put all her dreams and goals in them. She's a storyteller, like you. You'll know where to bury the necklace, Ellie. And you'll know how to make sure that she finds it. If you trust me, Ellie, the Stuart sapphires will at last find their way home.

He'd never left it up to her before. But he was trusting her, similar to how he'd asked her to trust him all those years ago, when they'd run away together.

Suddenly Eleanor knew exactly what to do so that the girl she was picturing would find the necklace and make everything right. Eleanor fetched her sketchbook from the easel and began to draw.

1

"I LOVED YOUR BOOK."

Those words were music to any writer's ears, and Nell MacPherson never tired of hearing them. She beamed a smile at the little girl standing in front of her table. "I'm so glad you did."

She took the copy of *It's All Good* the little girl held out to her and opened it to the title page. Her reading and signing at Pages, the bookstore—down the street from her sister Piper's Georgetown apartment—had run overtime. At one point, the line had spilled out into the street. The store's manager was thrilled, but Piper— who'd taken an extended morning break to attend—had glanced at her watch twice in the past fifteen minutes. She probably needed to head back to the office.

"What's your name?" Nell asked the little girl.

"Lissa. But I wish it was Ellie like the character in your book. Mommy says I look like her, but you do, too."

Lissa was right on both counts, Nell thought. They

both had Eleanor Campbell MacPherson's long blond hair and blue eyes.

"Mommy and I did some research. You're Ellie's great-great-great…" Lissa trailed off to glance up at her mother. "I forgot how many greats."

"Way too many," Nell said as she autographed the book. "I always say I'm Ellie and Angus's several-times-great-granddaughter."

"Did Ellie really draw all the pretty pictures for your story?"

"Yes. She was a talented artist. Every one of the illustrations came from her sketchbooks."

"And you live in her castle in New York," Lissa said.

"I grew up there, and I'm going back for a while to finish up another book." That hadn't been her original plan. The federal grant had given her a taste of what it was like to be totally independent, allowing her to travel across the country giving writing workshops to young children in inner city schools. For someone who'd been hovered over by a loving and overprotective family all her life, the past year had been a heady experience—one that she intended to build on.

But her sisters' recent adventures on the castle grounds—leading to the discovery of part of Eleanor Campbell's long-missing dowry—had caused Nell to question her plan of finding an apartment in New York City and finishing her second book there. Each of her siblings had discovered one of Eleanor's sapphire earrings. So wasn't it Nell's turn to find the necklace? Not that anyone in her family had suggested it. They had assumed she was returning home to settle in and take the teaching job that nearby Huntleigh College had offered her. But a week ago an anonymous letter had been delivered to her while she was teaching her last set of workshops in Louisville. The sender had used those exact words: *It's your turn.* Nell had known then that she had to return to the castle and find the rest of Eleanor's sapphires.

"Are you going to fall in love and kiss him beneath the stone arch that Angus built for Ellie?"

Nell reined in her thoughts.

"Lissa." The pretty woman standing behind the little girl put a hand on her shoulder and sent Nell an apologetic smile. "Thank Ms. MacPherson for signing your book."

"Thank you, Ms. MacPherson."

"Thank you for coming today, Lissa." Nell leaned a little closer. "Lots of people have kissed their true loves beneath that stone arch. My eldest sister, Adair, has recently become engaged to a man she kissed there. Cam Sutherland, a CIA agent. He's very handsome. And my aunt Vi is going to marry Cam's boss." Then she pointed to Piper who was standing near the door. "See that pretty woman over there?"

Lissa nodded.

"That's my other sister, Piper. She's a defense attorney here in D.C., and she just kissed her true love, FBI agent Duncan Sutherland, beneath the stone arch two weeks ago."

Lissa's eyes went wide. "And now they'll all live happily ever after, right?"

"That's the plan. In the meantime, my sister Adair and my aunt Vi are turning Castle MacPherson into a very popular place to fall in love and then have a wedding." She winked at the little girl. "When you're older and you find your true love, you might want to bring him up there."

"Can I, Mommy?" Lissa asked, a thrill in her voice. "Can I?"

"I don't see why not. But I can't see that happening for quite a while."

Lissa turned back to Nell. "What about you? Aren't you going to kiss your true love under the stones?"

"Someday," Nell said. But while her older sisters and her aunt might be ready for happy-ever-afters, Nell had much more she wanted to accomplish first. Finding Eleanor's sapphire necklace and finishing her second book were at the top of her list.

The instant Lissa's mother steered her daughter toward the checkout line, Piper crossed to Nell's table. "The Bronwell trial starts on Monday, and my boss is holding a press conference at five o'clock." Piper glanced at her watch. "I can treat you to a quick cup of coffee."

"No problem." Nell grabbed her purse and waved at the manager.

"You're great with the kids," Piper said. "They love talking to you about Eleanor and Angus."

She and Piper had nearly reached the door of the shop when a man rode his bike up over the curb and jumped off. A sense of déjà vu gripped Nell even before he had entered the store and she had read Instant Delivery on the insignia over his shirt pocket. The anonymous letter she'd received in Louisville had also been hand delivered.

"I have a letter for Nell MacPherson. Is she still here?" He spoke in a loud voice, his gaze sweeping the room.

"I'm Nell MacPherson."

The relief on his face was instantaneous. "Glad I didn't miss you. I was supposed to get here half an hour ago. The traffic today is worse than usual. If you'll just sign here."

As she signed, Nell's mind raced ahead. She hadn't told anyone in her family about the first letter. They would have wanted her to come home to the castle immediately so they could protect her. Worse still, now that her two sisters were involved with agents from the CIA and the FBI, they would have sent someone to hover over her. And the number one person they would have in mind would be Reid Sutherland.

Nell intended to avoid that at all cost. She also intended to avert their expectation that she and Reid live happily ever after. Just because her two sisters would soon wed Reid's two brothers didn't mean she had to marry the last triplet. No way was she ready for that fairy-tale ending.

This whole year had been about demonstrating to them that she could take care of herself. She took a quick look at the envelope held out to her. It was one of those standard-letter-sized ones used for overnight deliveries. The only return address was for the Instant Delivery office. She accepted it and tucked it under her arm.

"Aren't you going to open it?" Piper asked as they moved out onto the street.

"It's probably from my editor."

"Why would she send something to the bookstore? She'd simply call you, right? I think you should open it."

Curiosity and determination. Those were Piper's most outstanding qualities, and they served her well in her career. She wouldn't rest until she knew what was in the letter.

Nell pulled the tab. Inside was one page and the first four sentences matched the message in the first letter.

Your mission is to find the sapphire necklace that Eleanor Campbell stole from our family. Your sisters knew where to find the earrings. Now, it's your turn. I'll contact you and tell you how you can return the Stuart sapphires to their rightful owners.

Nell's gaze dropped to the last sentence. It was new, and an icy sliver of fear shot up her spine.

If you choose again to ignore your mission, someone in your family will die.

"ONE FOR THE ROAD," Lance Cabot said with a grin as he assumed the ancient fighting position, arms bent at the elbows and hands flexed.

Setting aside the file he was working on, Reid Sutherland stepped out from behind his desk and mirrored his adversary's stance. For seconds they moved in a small circle like dancers, retaking each other's measure.

"I can teach you the move," Reid offered as he had countless times before. Growing up as the oldest of triplet boys, he'd taken up martial arts as soon as his mother had allowed it. And he'd created the move by using his brothers for practice.

"Where's the fun in that? I think I've finally figured it out."

Reid blocked the kick aimed at his groin. "Maybe not."

They were evenly matched in height and weight, and Reid knew from experience that the baggy sweatshirt the man was wearing hid well-honed muscles. Reid was five years younger, so that gave him one advantage. And while four years at West Point and assignments in Bosnia and Iraq had kept his opponent fit, they hadn't provided the training in hand-to-hand combat that the Secret Service required of its agents. Another advantage for Reid. Plus Cabot's four-year stint in the United States Senate, not to mention a wife and two kids, could slow a man down.

A well-aimed foot grazed Reid's hip bone, making it sing. He feinted to the right, but the move didn't fool Cabot, and Reid had to dodge another kick. He blocked the next blow but felt it reverberate from his forearm to his shoulder. For two sweaty minutes, Cabot continued to attack, and Reid continued to defend himself.

Cabot had one major advantage. He was the vice president of the United States, and Reid's job was to protect him. Therefore, Reid kept his moves defensive. His office was not designed for hand-to-hand combat, but over the past year, that had meant squat to the VP. Thank God.

Reid feinted, ducked low and for the first time completely avoided Cabot's foot. The maneuver should have caused his opponent to stumble, but Lance Cabot merely shifted his weight and resumed his stance. "I like your moves."

"Ditto," Reid said as they continued their circular dance. He loved his job. Two things had drawn him to the Secret Service. First, the agency filled a need he'd had from an early age to protect those he cared about, and it allowed him to fulfill that need in a way that challenged him intellectually as well as physically.

Reid blocked a kick and danced to his right. Both of them liked a good fight, and neither wanted it to end yet. That was only one of the things that the two men shared. Like the VP, Reid knew what it was to balance family responsibility against that desire to push the envelope. He'd lived with it all of his life, and protecting the vice president had allowed him to push that envelope in ever new and exciting ways.

Keeping Cabot safe was first and foremost a mind game. It required the ability to foresee all possible scenarios in a given situation. Making sure that the VP could enjoy a Wednesday-night dinner with his wife in Georgetown posed almost as much of a challenge as his recent visit to the troops in Afghanistan. Plus the job offered the added bonus of protecting someone who was addicted to risk taking. Reid's boss had handpicked him to head up Cabot's Secret Service detail so that the VP's daredevil streak could be indulged—safely.

To date, those indulgences had included race-car driving, rock climbing and most recently skydiving. For Reid, it was the job of his dreams. And he'd learned that indulging the VP's danger addiction made him easier to manage when the threat might be all too real.

"We've been sparring like this for over a year. Are you ever going to show me your A game?" Cabot asked.

"Someday." Reid gave the man points: he wasn't even breathing heavily. "When it's no longer my job to protect you from serious injury, I'll be happy to oblige. Are you ever going to show me what you think my secret move is?"

"Soon," Cabot promised.

Unfortunately the clock was ticking down. Last night Reid had officially gone on vacation. Jenna Stanwick, an up-and-coming agent he'd been personally training for the past month, was heading up the protection unit in his place. She would keep watch over the VP and his family for the next two weeks while they vacationed in Martha's Vineyard. The Cabots were due to leave within the hour.

As if he too was aware that time was running out, Lance Cabot, quick as a cat, made his move, coming in low to grab Reid's arm. Reid countered it by pivoting, before he snaked his other arm around Cabot's neck and tossed him over his head. One of the chairs in front of his desk overturned and a paperweight clattered to the floor.

The door to the office shot open, and Jenna Stanwick strode into the room, gun drawn. With one sweeping glance she assessed the situation and reholstered her weapon. "Having fun, boys?"

"You didn't see this," Lance Cabot said as he got to his feet.

"See what?" Jenna asked.

Lance turned to Reid. "Maybe she will work out as your temporary replacement."

Shooting Jenna a look of approval, Reid said, "She will. She has four brothers. Plus I taught her my secret move. She'll teach it to you, if you want."

"Not on your life." But he studied Jenna with new interest. "How about if I practice on you, and you can tell me when I'm close?"

Jenna smiled at him. "I'd love to, but you'll have to check the schedule your wife has mapped out. It looks pretty full to me."

Once Jenna had stepped out and closed the door, Reid righted the overturned chair and offered it to Cabot. "You are going to have a good time with your wife and sons. Even if none of the planned activities offer much of an adrenaline rush."

Cabot grinned at him. "Oh, there'll be adrenaline rushes—they'll just be different. Isn't it time you explored the adventures you can have once you marry and have children?"

Reid raised both hands in mock surrender. "No thanks. I'm not cut out for family responsibilities." He'd decided that a long time ago, during the slew of repercussions that had followed his father's arrest for embezzlement.

With a grin, Cabot sank into the chair. "You just need the right woman to change your mind." He waved a hand at the photos displayed on the credenza beside Reid's desk. "Or maybe your brothers could do the job, seeing as they've both found that special woman in the past few months." He dropped his gaze to the duffel bag at the foot of Reid's desk. "For a man who's dead set on avoiding the whole marriage-and-family thing, aren't you running a huge risk spending your vacation up at that castle with those magic stones?"

Reid narrowed his eyes. "Who says I'm going to Castle MacPherson?"

Cabot's grin widened. "Elementary. Really elementary. I don't have to be Sherlock Holmes to figure out you're headed there. Not with the publicity your brothers have received lately. Each of them has been involved in the discovery of part of the long-missing Stuart sapphires. But the necklace is still lost. My bet is that sibling rivalry alone is pulling at you. I'm surprised that some enterprising reporter hasn't sought you out for an interview."

Reid's eyes narrowed. "My brothers have kept a very

low profile. You only know the extent of their involvement because I told you." So far, any publicity Cam and Duncan had garnered had centered on the romantic side of their adventures with Adair and Piper MacPherson, a slant that was encouraged because of the castle's wedding business.

Cabot raised both hands, palms outward. "Just saying. Last night one of the cable news channels did a Cliffs Notes summary of pretty much everything you've told me about unearthing the first two earrings."

Reid had caught the broadcast. The correspondent had laid out a coherent time line, starting with Adair finding the first earring after lightning had struck the stone arch, and ending with Piper and Duncan's discovery of the second earring in one of the caves on the castle grounds. The reporter's narrative had focused on the drama—the threats to the young women's lives. The villain who'd tried to kill Adair was in jail, and Deanna Lewis—the woman who'd subdued Duncan with a Taser shot and then had abducted Piper—was in a coma in a hospital in Albany. So far the press hadn't latched onto the fact that, for six months prior to finding the first earring, someone had been paying undetected nocturnal visits to the castle. Cam's theory was that the visits had been triggered by a feature article in the *New York Times* linking Eleanor's dowry to the sapphires that Mary Stuart had worn at her coronation. The piece had stirred up a whirlwind of interest in the missing jewels, and it had also enormously helped Adair and Viola MacPherson launch their wedding destination business at the castle.

"The anchor mentioned the fact that the youngest MacPherson sister had yet to pay a visit to the castle since the first earring was discovered," Cabot said. "The implication was that, when she did, the necklace might be found. If her sisters' experiences are any indication, she'll need some protection, so it's not a leap to think that the speculation might extend to you eventually."

Reid said nothing. He wasn't worried about the media getting around to him. But the cable newscast had certainly heightened the nagging worry he'd had about Nell. Cabot was thinking along the same lines that Reid was. Nell's two sisters had been lucky enough to find Eleanor Campbell's missing earrings. It definitely wasn't a stretch that anyone who wanted to gain possession of the necklace would be keeping an eye on Nell.

He intended to do just that himself.

Lance Cabot laughed. "That deadpan look works well in a poker game. And it may work with the media. But I know you. You're going to take a shot at finding that necklace. That's the real reason why you're sending me off with the very capable Jenna Stanwick."

Cabot was right about that, too. Reid *was* going to take a shot at finding the necklace. That was the second reason why his duffel was packed and waiting. He'd learned that Nell was heading to the castle on Sunday after her book signing today in Georgetown and a few days with her sister Piper. By joining her, he could kill two birds with one stone. Make sure she was safe and find the necklace.

The damn thing had always fascinated him.

The image flashed into his mind of the first time he'd seen the painting of Eleanor wearing her sapphires. He and his brothers had been ten, and their newly divorced mother, Professor Beth Sutherland, had made arrangements with A. D. MacPherson to research Beth's first historical novel in the castle's library. Part of the arrangement she'd negotiated had allowed her to bring her triplet sons along to the castle every day. Thus had begun a long summer of playdates that he and Cam and Duncan had shared with the MacPherson sisters.

Of course the oil painting had only hinted at the beauty of the jewels, but he'd felt something as he'd stood beneath the portrait that day and had listened to the story of Angus and Eleanor's flight from Scotland to the New World. The older girls had let little Nell do most of the talking, and all through the recital, Reid hadn't been able to take his eyes off the jewels.

Tradition held that this artwork in the main parlor was Eleanor's wedding portrait, and the priceless sapphires were her dowry. But after her death there was no proof of their existence. Reid imagined that her children and grandchildren had searched the castle thoroughly, but they'd never found the sapphires. The long-missing "treasure" had become the focus of many of the games he and his brothers had played with the MacPherson sisters that summer.

It was on that day, looking at the painting, that he'd made a promise to himself that one day he would find Eleanor's dowry. Of course life had interrupted. When the summer had ended, their mother had taken them back to Chicago and resumed her teaching responsibilities. But Reid had never forgotten the jewels or the story that Nell had woven about her ancestors.

Seven years ago, he and his brothers had returned to the castle for a brief visit on the day that their mother had married A. D. MacPherson beneath the castle's legendary stone arch. That had been the last time he had crossed the MacPherson girls' paths. He and Cam and Duncan had been seniors in college and totally focused on their careers. Cam had already interviewed at the CIA. Duncan had his sights set on working in the behavioral science division of the FBI, and Reid's own goal had been to land a job in the Secret Service. None of those careers left much time for family. So even though they were technically stepbrothers and stepsisters, it hadn't been until this summer that their lives had intersected again.

A tap sounded on the door, and Lance Cabot rose from his chair. "My vacation adventure calls." At the door, he turned back. "Good luck finding the sapphires. But in two weeks, I expect you back on the job. By then I will have figured out your secret move."

"Not worried."

"You should be."

Reid could hear Cabot's laughter even after he shut the door behind him. But he didn't smile. His conversation with the VP had only increased what his instincts had been telling him ever since Piper and Duncan had found the second earring. Nell could be in serious danger.

The cable news correspondent hadn't spent much time at all on Deanna Lewis. But Reid's family had been digging into her background for the past ten days. She'd been born and raised in London, the only daughter of Mary and Douglas Lewis. Deanna's mother had died when she was three, her father when she was a freshman in college. She'd been working as a freelance photographer when she'd sold the senior editor of *Architectural Digest* on the idea of doing a feature article on Castle MacPherson. In short, she was everything she'd represented herself to be when she'd appeared at the castle that day and abducted Piper.

And Deanna still had a partner out there. Someone who not only wanted the sapphires but who believed he had a right to them. Deanna Lewis had claimed that the sapphires had never been Eleanor's dowry, that she'd stolen them when she'd fled Scotland with Angus. It all boiled down to a priceless fortune in jewels and someone who was willing to do anything to lay hands on them.

That put the MacPherson sisters in serious danger. Fortunately his brothers had been on the scene when the worst of the trouble had erupted, and they were each sticking like glue to the older sisters. Cam had Adair with him in Scotland working with A.D. and their mother to see if they could find out who might claim the sapphires on that end. His brother Duncan was keeping a close watch on Piper now that she was working on a high-profile defense case in D.C.

That left Nell. Frowning, Reid picked up his pen and drew it through his fingers. So far the danger had been focused on the castle. But that could change. The sense of urgency that had been plaguing him for over a week now bumped up a notch when his cell blasted out his brother Cam's ringtone. His brother seldom called with good news. But he was in Scotland. It couldn't be about Nell. Taking the call, he spoke the standard phrase he and his brothers always used.

"Problem or favor?" And he willed it to be the latter.

2

"Neither," Cam said. "And this is a conference call. Duncan's on the line, too. Mom asked me to call."

Cam's tone had most of Reid's tension easing.

"Congratulations, Cam," Duncan said. "Usually Mom calls Reid to pass on the messages. Clearly the pecking order has changed."

Grinning now, Reid leaned back in his chair. The fact that their mom usually called him first was something that his brothers had razzed him about since they'd gone away to college. She'd been a very busy professor then, and since he'd been the firstborn of the triplets, she'd put him at the top of her phone tree. The habit had stuck. "Let me add my congratulations, too," Reid said. "I'm perfectly willing to hand that particular torch over to you, Cam."

"Of course, it could be a case of *out of sight, out of mind*," Duncan said. "Cam's over there with her in Scotland. You're not."

That was true enough. Their mother had gained access to the library at the old Campbell estate that Eleanor had fled from with Angus so long ago. Beth was interested in uncovering the story that had led up to their flight to the New World to use in her latest historical novel. With the added information Deanna Lewis had brought to the table, they were all interested. "How can either of you be sure that Mom hasn't already called me?" Reid asked.

The beat of silence gave Reid great satisfaction. He leaned back in his chair.

"She hasn't," Cam said firmly.

Duncan laughed. "Keep thinking that, Cam."

"I know she hasn't called him yet because Adair and I were just with her when she discovered it in the library. Many of the books there were damaged or destroyed in a fire about six months ago, but leave it to Mom to dig up something."

Reid set down his pen. "What did she find?"

"Yeah." The teasing tone had disappeared from Duncan's voice. "Is it something that will help us identify the person Deanna Lewis was working with when she attacked Piper?"

"I'm hoping it will give us a start," Cam said. "Mom came across an old family Bible with part of the Campbell family tree sketched on the inside cover page. Eleanor's name is right there. She had two older sisters, Gwendolen and Ainslee." Cam spelled the names. "Both married and had children, and we can trace their descendants until around 1900. It's giving us some names to look at. Adair and I are going to start checking them out."

"Did one of them marry a Lewis?" Duncan asked.

"No," Cam said.

"Any more information on how the Stuart sapphires came into the Campbells' possession?" Reid asked. "If we knew that, we might have some idea why someone else believes to have a claim on them."

"Nothing yet," Cam said. "We're thinking that you might have a better chance of nailing down that part on your end."

"How do you figure?" Reid asked.

"I was here right after Adair found the first earring. Duncan and Piper found the second earring together. It's up to you to find the necklace. Along with Nell, of course. That should smoke out Deanna Lewis's partner, and you can get the story from him. Or her."

"Got to say, I'm siding with Cam on that one," Duncan said.

That was a new wrinkle, Reid thought. From the time they were very young, Duncan had made it a habit to stay silent and not side with either of them. The fact that his brothers' scenario matched up with the one presented on cable news only increased his worry that whoever was behind the attack on Piper and Duncan was thinking along the same lines. Nell might very well become their next target.

"Unless you are too afraid of those stones—and of falling for Nell," Cam said. "Oh, right. I forgot. You and Nell have been a done deal since you were ten."

Reid grimaced but said nothing. His brothers had teased him mercilessly that summer because he'd made it his priority to protect her.

"Afraid?" Duncan chuckled. "Not our brother. But our fearless leader is really going to hate following in our footsteps. Nell's visiting Piper right now in Georgetown. They're at Nell's book signing. But she's planning on going up to the castle Sunday afternoon. Daryl assigned himself to be there for the wedding Vi's handling this weekend and all next week. Cam has beefed up the security system on the castle, and Sheriff Skinner is using local volunteers to patrol the grounds. But Nell needs more protection once she gets to the castle."

That was the real reason behind the phone call from his brothers, Reid thought. They'd double-teamed him, and they'd known what buttons to push. Find the treasure and protect the youngest sister.

"I'll think about it." No need to tell them that he'd already decided to spend his time off at the castle.

"You have to do more than think about it. This person is dangerous," Cam said.

Duncan laughed. "He's pulling your leg, Cam. He's not just thinking about it. He's already got his bags packed. And I'm signing off. I'm getting another call."

There was a beat of silence before Cam said, "Duncan's right, isn't he? You do have your bags packed. Did A.D. already call you and tell you to get up there?"

"I'll never tell." Reid thoroughly enjoyed the annoyance he was hearing in Cam's voice. "That's why they call us Secret Service agents," he said and ended the call.

Reaching into the top drawer of his desk, he brought out the copy of Nell's book, *It's All Good*. Curious, he'd bought it a year ago when it had first been published, and when he read it, he'd thoroughly enjoyed it. She'd been six when he had stood beneath the portrait, and he had been as transfixed by the story she'd woven as by the sapphires. Even then she had had a gift for narrative, and in her book, she managed to bring Angus and Eleanor's story vividly to life. Despite the fact that it was a children's story, it had gripped his interest and his imagination right to the end.

Of course he'd known the ending ahead of time. The standard fairy-tale myth. True love would triumph over all and last forever.

Right.

In Reid's experience, nothing lasted forever, and true love was a rare commodity, if it existed at all. His mother's first marriage was testimony to that because it had nearly destroyed her. It might have destroyed them all.

Reid set down Nell's well-crafted fairy tale and let his mind drift back to the night when the police and the FBI had come to their home and arrested their father, David Fedderman. Reid and his brothers had been nine. Gradually they had learned the details behind the arrest. For several years, their father had been running a very successful Ponzi scheme in the investment firm that his grandfather had founded. Being born to wealth and privilege hadn't been enough for David Fedderman. He'd used his charm and intelligence to build a financial house of cards that had tripled the worth of Fedderman Investments.

At least on paper.

Duncan, the behavioral analyst in the family, believed their father was addicted to the thrill of running a con, and living on the edge had been worth more to him than wealth or family. Reid glanced down at Nell's book and wondered if David Fedderman had ever loved his mother at all. What he did know was that she had loved him, and he had broken her heart.

The image of his father being handcuffed and dragged from their home was indelibly imprinted on Reid's mind. He and his brothers had stood in a protective line in front of their mother, and that was symbolically where they'd remained during the turbulent years that had followed.

The Feddermans had sued for the triplets' custody, and what had begun with their father's arrest had changed all of their lives.

On the advice of her attorney, their mother had continued to pursue her doctoral studies. She landed a job teaching at a small college on the outskirts of Chicago, while Reid and his brothers had pitched in to help. Reid had been the idea man and organizer, and he'd been able to turn to Duncan for analysis and Cam to carry out any missions. Together they'd made sure that their mother had time for her academic pursuits.

In the preteen years that followed, Reid and his brothers had been as prone to mischief and getting into scrapes as most boys their age. More so. If two heads were better than one, three active and imaginative minds could hatch some adventures that, at the very least, might have distracted their mother. When they'd gotten into some of their worst scrapes, he'd run interference in an effort to protect them all. Perhaps because of that, she'd come to confide in him. The saddest thing she had ever told him was that she'd not only loved their father very much but believed that he'd loved her, too.

But their "true" love hadn't been enough.

One thing he knew for sure. What had happened had made his mother gun-shy with men. In fact, it was a key reason behind her love of research and choice to steep herself in scholarships and writing.

The triplets all believed that their mother and A. D. MacPherson initially fell in love during the summer that she'd first visited Castle MacPherson, but she'd waited over a decade to trust in the idea of true love again.

And though Reid had recently seen his two brothers take that risky fall and wished them well, Reid didn't have the time or the inclination to follow in their footsteps. He loved his career, and he was fully capable of allowing his work to consume him.

In that sense he believed that he was like both his father and his mother. He liked it that way, even though he'd seen up close what total focus on a career had done to his father, and the price his family had paid. He was determined not to risk boxing himself into the same position.

Still he had to hand it to Nell: in her book, she'd done an excellent job of making the myth seem real. As he flipped through the pages again, he noted the illustrations—the stone arch and other landmarks that surrounded the castle. He'd read in an article that the illustrations had been drawn by Eleanor herself. Nell's ancestor had the same talent Nell had for capturing significant details on the page. Studying them brought vividly to mind the little fairy-tale princess of a girl that he'd done his best to protect that long-ago summer.

He fervently wished that was the only image of Nell that lingered in his mind. But there was another one that he couldn't quite shake loose. At their parents' wedding, she'd still looked a bit like a fairy-tale princess with her long blond hair. But she hadn't been a little girl anymore. She'd been eighteen, just on the brink of womanhood, and she'd been beautiful.

Stunning actually. Her resemblance to Eleanor Campbell MacPherson had been striking. He'd caught himself looking at her more than once during the brief wedding ceremony, and when he'd met her gaze, for a moment he hadn't been able to see anyone or anything else. And he'd felt…well, the only way he could describe it was a kind of recognition—a knowledge that she was the one for him. It was as if they stood alone beneath the stone arch, and he'd wanted her with an intensity that he'd never felt before or since.

Later when he returned to college and the demands of finishing his senior year, he'd convinced himself that what he'd felt was a fluke, a onetime thing that had been triggered by the emotions of the day and his twenty-two-year-old hormones. Still he'd been careful to avoid Nell. A pretty easy task given the demands of his career.

But once the sapphires started popping up, he'd known that he would see Nell again—and he was enough of a Scot to believe that perhaps it was destined.

And if what he'd felt beneath the stones hadn't been a fluke?

Well, he wasn't twenty-two anymore, and he'd always been able to handle Nell. As he recalled, she'd been eager to please and meticulous about following orders, so he didn't expect any problems in that regard.

Rising from his desk, he tucked the book into his duffel bag. But the ringtone on his cell had him crossing back to his desk quickly. It was Duncan. Why was he calling again when his earlier mission had been accomplished?

Unless…

"Problem or favor?" Reid asked.

"A big problem," Duncan replied, his tone grim.

3

As a FICTION WRITER, Nell knew that a good story always began on the day the trouble started. There was no mistaking that the letter with the threat to her family meant trouble.

If you choose to ignore your mission, someone in your family will die.

The numbing chill that had streaked through her when she'd first read the words hadn't surprised her. Neither had the fear she felt, fluttering like a trapped bird in her throat. Those were standard reactions any of her fictional characters might have felt. But the spurts of anger and excitement had been both unexpected and helpful. Because of those feelings, she'd been able to keep her smile in place, and get herself and her sister Piper halfway down the block and seated in the little sidewalk café before she handed over the letter.

Now, Piper, ever the lawyer, was reading it for at least the third time. Nell suppressed an urge to pinch herself to see if she was just imagining it all.

The setting couldn't have been more perfect if she'd been writing it. The morning sun was already high in the cloudless blue sky, the temperature was in the low eighties and the humidity tolerable. The sidewalks were bustling with happy shoppers and tourists. The whole lovely scene offered a stark contrast to the threat in the letter.

"I don't like this," Piper said. Then she read the message again, this time out loud.

Nell didn't like it, either. Hearing the threat helped her to focus on the fact that this wasn't some story she was making up. No need to pinch herself; this was real. And it was up to her to do something about it.

Excitement sparked again. She'd spent her entire life reading, imagining and writing stories, and now she was going to live one of her own. Wasn't that just what she wanted? Where would the adventure take her? Would she have the courage and the know-how to do what any one of her fictional heroines would?

One thing she knew for certain. No one was going to hurt anyone in her family—not if she could prevent it.

The waiter set down two chocolate and caramel Frappuccino drinks. Nell took a long sip of hers. She'd learned a long time ago that chocolate helped smooth over life's rough patches. Not that she'd had very many. As the youngest of three sisters, her life had always run pretty smoothly. She'd been a baby when her mother had died, and their father had turned into a recluse. So she hadn't known either of them long enough to really miss them. Then their aunt Vi had moved in with them, and Nell had always thought of Viola MacPherson as her mother.

People had always taken care of Nell. Adair had been the idea person, and based on her inspirations, Nell would invent stories that the three of them could act out during playtime. When Nell's plotlines had landed the MacPherson girls in trouble, Adair landed on her feet and thought of a way out. Or Piper, always the negotiator, would find a way to fix things with their aunt.

It wasn't until Nell went to college that she'd had to solve problems entirely on her own. Her goal from the time she was little had been to become a published writer and tell the stories she was always spinning in her mind. On the surface, the fact that she'd signed a publishing contract for her first book within a year of graduation might look like pretty smooth sailing. But she'd worked hard to achieve it.

The federal grant she had landed had allowed her to visit cities across the United States, offering writing classes to children and promoting her book at the same time. Several of the schools she'd visited had added *It's All Good* to their required reading lists, and they were passing the word on to other schools and libraries. Adair called what she was doing "networking."

The signing at Pages bookstore earlier today had been the last stop. It had only stalled her return to the castle by a few days. How could she have known that the delay could put those she loved in jeopardy?

"My best guess is that whoever sent this is the person Deanna Lewis was working with. Or at least someone who shares her belief that Eleanor did not have a right to the sapphires." Piper glanced up and met Nell's eyes. "Agreed?"

"Yes."

"One thing I don't get," Piper said. "Why did they send this letter to you? You've been traveling the country. And Adair and I have a proven track record. We each found one of the earrings."

They think it's my turn, Nell thought. What she said was, "The two of you stirred up quite a bit of publicity. Anyone paying attention knows that Adair is now engaged to a CIA agent, and you've hooked up with an FBI profiler. I don't come with that kind of baggage."

Piper studied her for a moment, before she nodded. "Okay. Makes sense. But another thing puzzles me." She tapped a finger on the last sentence. "Why do they say 'if you refuse your mission *again*'?"

Guilt stabbed at Nell, and she felt heat rise to her cheeks. She hadn't told Piper about the first letter. Whatever excuses she'd come up with in Louisville for keeping it a secret vaporized the instant she'd read that last sentence. She took a deep breath. "I received a letter very similar to that one a week ago."

Piper stared at her for two beats. "You what?"

Nell dug into her purse, pulled out the letter and laid it next to the other one so that Piper could read it. "I put it in a plastic bag, like the evidence bags they use on TV shows. Any fingerprints, including mine, are preserved. You can see it's the same message—except for the last line."

And the last line in the second letter was the kicker.

Piper frowned down at the first letter. "Why didn't you tell me or Aunt Vi immediately? We could have arranged for someone to protect you."

"That's exactly why I didn't tell anyone," Nell said, lifting her chin. "The last thing I wanted was for everyone to descend on Louisville. I'm not a child who needs to be rescued anymore. Besides, it could have been just a prank."

Piper took her hand and spoke in a tone that Nell remembered too well from her childhood. "Pranks have to be taken seriously when a fortune in sapphires is involved. Adair and I were both nearly killed."

Nell raised her free hand, palm out. "Point taken." The best way to handle Piper was to pretend to go along. But there was no way she was going to miss this chance to prove to them that she no longer needed to be sheltered and protected. They'd always taken care of her. Now she'd take care of them.

"It's going to be all right," Piper said.

Nell barely kept herself from rolling her eyes. How many times had she heard that sentence while she was growing up? She took a second sip of icy chocolate-flavored coffee and mimicked Piper's tone. "Yes, it is. I'll leave for the castle by noon."

Piper's gaze narrowed. "No, you won't. It's too dangerous. You'll stay here with me until we figure out what to do."

"I'll put all of us in even more danger if I don't go. I have to find the necklace, and we're not going to find it across the street in your apartment. Everyone agrees that Eleanor must have hidden the necklace somewhere on the grounds of Castle MacPherson."

"That's the problem. *Everyone* does agree it's there. Since the word leaked out that Duncan and I found a second sapphire earring in the caves, the treasure seekers are coming out of the woodwork, and the castle is getting more visitors and trespassers than usual. It's too dangerous up there."

Nell's eyes narrowed. "But it's not too dangerous for Aunt Vi or for Adair, who's coming back from Scotland soon. Or for you. I don't suppose it's too dangerous for Duncan or Cam Sutherland, either."

"Cam is CIA. Duncan is FBI. They're professionals. You're not."

Biting her tongue, Nell reminded herself of her strategy. *Pretend to go along.*

Piper released her hand and gave it a pat. "I'm calling Duncan. I wrote down the name of the delivery service that brought this to the bookstore. He'll know how to trace it, and he has a friend who works for the D.C. police, a Detective Nelson. He can check for fingerprints. Then Duncan can let both his brothers know about this, while I call Aunt Vi at the castle. She'll make sure the word gets passed on to Adair and Dad over in Scotland. We'll handle it. Don't you worry about a thing."

Don't you worry about a thing. Another familiar sentence from her childhood. In fact, the whole scenario, with her family sidelining her and solving her problems, had been the story of her life.

Until now.

Nell squared her shoulders and met her sister's eyes. "You *can't* handle this for me. I know that's what everyone has done all my life, but whoever wrote that letter wants *me* to find Eleanor's necklace. I was planning on looking for it anyway. Adair and Aunt Vi found the first earring in the stone arch. You and Duncan found the second one in those caves we used to play in. So it's my turn to find the rest of Eleanor's dowry. That's the way the story is supposed to go."

She paused to beam a smile at Piper. "Once I have the necklace, this person will contact me, and we'll find out just what he or she wants. I'm personally interested in discovering why they think they have a claim on the sapphires. Aren't you?"

Piper had retrieved her phone and now scowled at

her. "This isn't one of your stories where you can plan out the happy ending. The person who wrote this could be very dangerous, and he planned this meticulously. He knew you had that book signing today. He's probably watching us even now."

Nell ignored the chill that shot up her spine. "I know." That would be exactly the way she would write it. "There's this scene in an old Clint Eastwood movie, *Absolute Power,* where his daughter asks him to meet her at this sidewalk café right here in D.C. The FBI wants to arrest him, and two snipers are waiting to take him out. He escapes, of course."

"Of course he does. He's Clint Eastwood. And at the risk of repeating myself, you're not." Then Piper narrowed her eyes. "And what do you know about snipers? You write children's stories."

"Doesn't mean I don't read grown-up ones. My point is that it's not any more dangerous at the castle than it might be right here. There could be a sniper taking aim at us right now."

"All the more reason why you need protection. Ever since that article brought the missing sapphires to the public's attention, there are a lot of people, including some professional thieves, who want to get their hands on those jewels." Piper tapped a finger on the last line of the second letter. "This is a clear death threat."

"Yes." The chill Nell experienced was colder than it had been before. She firmly ignored it as she leaned closer and tapped her finger on the same line. "Piper, the writer is not threatening me. He's threatening all of you, if I don't find the necklace. So I'm going up to the castle, and I will find it. You're not going to talk me out of it."

"I'm calling Duncan." Piper punched in numbers.

While Piper relayed the situation to Duncan Sutherland, Nell studied her sister's face and delighted in the way it softened and then began to glow as she spoke to him. No one believed in the power of the stones more than Nell did. But as a writer, she also knew that the power of the legend didn't cover all scenarios. Her parents were a prime example of that. They had found true love, but her mother's death had cut their time short and had devastated her father. Life gave no guarantees.

That meant that she had to be very careful about the way she handled Reid Sutherland.

She reached for her drink and took a long swallow. She and Reid went back a very long time to the magical summer he was ten and she was six. She and her sisters had played games every single day with the Sutherland triplets, games that had opened up all kinds of story possibilities in her mind—posse and sheriff, pirates and treasure, good and evil.

That was the summer that she'd fallen in love with Reid. From a six-year-old's perspective, he'd been the personification of all the storybook princes and adventure heroes she'd ever read about. Whenever the games they had played had gotten too dangerous or too challenging, he'd been her protector or her champion. Guinevere couldn't have had a better Lancelot. Cinderella couldn't have met a more handsome prince at the ball. Princess Leia couldn't have fought side by side with a more daring Han Solo.

When that summer had ended and Reid had disappeared from her life, he'd remained the hero in all the stories she'd woven for years to come. Knowing full well that, at six, she'd seen Reid Sutherland through rose-colored Disney-movie glasses.

A dozen years later when his mother had married her father beneath Angus and Eleanor's stone arch, the way she'd seen Reid had been entirely different. He was no longer just a good-looking boy. He'd turned into an incredibly attractive man. While their parents recited vows, she found her gaze returning to him again and again. She hadn't been able to stop herself. Even now, years later, she could easily conjure up the image of that lean, raw-boned face, the tousled dark hair. The full, firm mouth.

And she could still remember what she'd felt— dryness in her throat, rapid beat to her heart and the strangest melting sensation in her body. When he had glanced over and met her gaze, she'd felt that flutter right beneath her heart, and she'd been certain that she was falling in love with him all over again.

A mistake that could be excused in a naive eighteen-year-old who'd never felt such strong attraction for a man before. Thank heavens she'd never let him or anyone else know that he'd twice been the object of her heart's desire. He always thought of her as a child; someone he felt indulgent toward. Someone he had to go out of his way to protect from harm. After their parents' wedding, he'd made his feelings for her quite clear when he'd kissed her on the nose and called her "my new little stepsister."

Those words had crushed her heart, and inspired by one of Adair's plans, she'd put pen to paper and created a very different narrative about Reid Sutherland.

Nell took another sip of her icy coffee as the memory poured into her mind in vivid detail. It had been midnight when Adair and Piper had come to her room and awakened her. The wedding guests had long-ago departed, and their aunt Vi was sound asleep. Piper had swiped a bottle of champagne, and they'd gone out to the stone arch, the way they'd done so many times growing up. But with cola or tea in their childhood years.

Beneath the stones, they'd shared their goals and dreams and secrets. More than that, at Adair's suggestion, they'd written down those goals and put them in their mother's old jewelry box. As children, they'd tucked the box behind some stones that were loose to tap into the power that resided there. Back then, Adair had come up with the idea of burying all their secret goals in the stones. The theory had been that, if the stone arch had the power to bring true lovers together, it might also have the power to make other dreams come true. Even the very practical-minded Piper had decided that it was worth a shot.

Nell had continued to tuck her goals into the box even after her sisters had gone away to college. Since it was divided into three compartments, it was perfect for their purpose. Adair had insisted from the beginning that they each use a different color paper to ensure privacy. Piper had chosen blue, Adair yellow and Nell had selected pink.

On the night of the wedding, it was Adair, of course, who had suggested that they cap the celebration by writing out their most secret and thrilling sexual fantasy. Perhaps Nell's fantasy had evolved as it did because she had been standing in the exact same spot when her gaze had locked with Reid's during the ceremony. Maybe because the memory of what she'd felt was still so fresh—that rush of desire, the glorious wave of heat and the flutter right beneath her heart. Or perhaps it had been the champagne. But, of course, her sexual fantasy had involved Reid Sutherland.

And that night she'd been creatively inspired. Her best story ideas came to her while she was actually writing. The physical acts of running her pen over the paper or her fingers atop the keyboard tapped into her creative imagination the way nothing else did. And she'd certainly tapped into it that night. Nell had been eighteen, a freshman in college, and what she'd written went far beyond her limited experience. The details of those original fantasies were a bit fuzzy now. But the setting she'd chosen and the broader picture were perfectly clear.

No longer was Reid the romantic hero of her childhood fairy tales. No, indeed. In her fantasy, seduction had been her goal. And she'd chosen the most romantic setting she could think of—Eleanor's garden. Over the years, she'd had plenty of time to embroider and expand on her original ideas. And those scenarios had been fueling her dreams, especially since the Sutherland men had reentered her sisters' lives.

Of course what she'd felt that day could have been a onetime thing. But working against that theory was the fact that every time she relived it in her mind, she felt the same things all over again. No one before or since had ever made her want with such intensity. With that feeling of inevitability.

The question was, when she finally met Reid again, what would happen next? Each time she asked it, a fresh thrill rippled through her system. As a writer, it was the question she always wanted foremost in her readers' minds. It was what made them turn the page. And she found that the more she thought about it, the more she wanted to turn the page in her own life and discover what would happen.

Just thinking about it had her reaching again for her drink to cool down her system. She hadn't seen Reid since their parents' wedding day. His job heading up the vice president's security team made him a very busy man. Still she had no doubt that they would meet again sometime soon, and she would have the opportunity to turn her fantasies into reality. And she'd made preparations.

A heady thrill moved through her at the thought.

"Earth to Nell."

Piper's words made Nell shift her gaze to the letters Piper was placing in her briefcase. Giving herself a mental shake, Nell refocused on the fact that she was currently involved in a much more pressing narrative.

"Duncan wants to see both letters. We'll take a taxi to Reid's office, and he'll meet us there." She left two bills on the table to pay for their coffees.

"Reid's office? Why do we have to go there?" Nell asked.

"It's halfway between Duncan's office and here. Plus Duncan says Reid's on vacation, and he's going to the castle with you."

In her mind, Nell pictured a guardian angel swooping down on her. "I don't need anyone to protect me. I can handle this."

"Don't be silly." Punching another number into her phone, Piper moved quickly toward the curb. "Abe, I'm going to be a little late for work. Family emergency."

Family emergency? Nell frowned. Nell grabbed one

last swallow of chocolate-laced caffeine and rose from her seat.

Piper turned back to her. "The best place to catch a taxi is at the opposite corner. Follow me."

Then she stepped in between two parked cars to wait for traffic to clear.

A horn blast drew Nell's attention. A few stores down, a dark sedan was blocking traffic. The driver behind him demonstrated his displeasure by leaning on the horn again. Piper glanced at the noise also and then turned her attention back to her phone call.

Nell had only taken one step when a woman came up to her. "Ms. MacPherson? You are Nell MacPherson, right?"

"Yes, I am."

The woman was a tall brunette in her early fifties who looked as if she could have stepped right off the cover of a high-end fashion magazine. "I missed your signing, and I was wondering if you could autograph a book for my granddaughter?"

"Of course."

While the woman fished in her bag for the book and a pen, Nell heard the horn again and the sound of a motor revving. She caught a blur of movement out of the corner of her eye. The image of the dark sedan shooting forward had barely registered, when she realized that Piper was directly in its path. Fear flashed so brightly in her mind that for a moment she was blinded. Pure instinct had her pushing past the woman and racing toward the street.

Piper seemed so far away, the sound of the car so close. Nell felt as if she was moving in slow motion, the car on fast-forward. She slammed into her sister, grabbing her around the waist and using Nell's momentum to hurl them both forward. They were airborne for a second. Holding tight to Piper, Nell twisted so that she took the impact on her side when they tumbled onto the pavement. Then with every ounce of energy she had, she rolled, dragging her sister with her. Hot wind seared her cheek, and she smelled burning rubber as the dark sedan whipped past and sped up the street.

"Nell? Are you all right?"

Pain was singing through every bone in her body, but Nell managed a smile as she opened her eyes and looked into Piper's. "I'm fine. You?"

"Yeah," Piper said. "Thanks to you."

"He was crazy," a man said as he helped both of them to their feet.

Piper ran her hands over her sister. "You're sure you're all right?"

"I'm better than I was a moment ago." Nell didn't want to ever replay those few seconds in her mind again.

For a moment Piper just held on to her sister's hands. There was a look in her eyes that Nell had never seen before. Surprise?

"You saved my life," Piper said. "I guess you were right about it being just as dangerous here as at the castle."

"It's all good," Nell said as she pulled her sister close and just held on to her for a minute.

"I wrote down his license plate number," a woman said. "It looked to me like he wanted to run you over, young lady. You should report him."

"I will." Pulling away from Nell, Piper took the slip of paper.

"I called 9-1-1," another woman said. "They're sending the police to take a report."

Glancing around, Nell noted that they'd attracted quite a little crowd. On the edge of it, she saw a young man pushing forward. As he reached her, she saw that he had an envelope in his hand. "Sorry, lady," he said. "The guy in that car gave me this to deliver to you after you left the café. He paid me fifty bucks and told me to wait until you crossed the street. I had no idea he was going to try to run you down."

"Thanks," Nell said. But it wasn't her the driver had been aiming for. It had been Piper.

"Let me open it for you," Piper said, then pulled out her phone to call Duncan once more.

"No." This was her story, and if she'd had any lingering doubts about that, they vanished as she read the message on the letter inside.

You have forty-eight hours to find the sapphire necklace, or you run the risk of losing another member of your family.

4

HORNS BLASTED AS Reid made an illegal left-hand turn that would cut five minutes off his trip to Piper MacPherson's apartment in Georgetown, near the latest Stuart sapphires crime scene. Now if he could just make it through the next few traffic lights. He cut off a car in the right lane, pressed his foot on the gas and shot through a yellow one. Duncan's ringtone had him grabbing his cell just as he headed into one of D.C.'s traffic circles.

"I'm still ten minutes out," Duncan said.

"I'll be there in less than five." Reid slammed on his brakes as the car in front of him slowed. "I'll let you know the second I arrive." He dropped his cell on the passenger seat and concentrated on snaking his way through the traffic.

He should have told Duncan to have the two women wait for him where they were, as soon as he'd first heard about the first two threatening letters. Why hadn't he? He seldom had to second-guess himself. His success in the Secret Service depended on him being right the first time.

But this particular scenario simply hadn't occurred to him. The writer of the letters had threatened Nell's family if she didn't locate the rest of Eleanor's sapphires and hand them over to their rightful owner. It was a good ploy. It would have probably scared her into taking a shot at finding the necklace ASAP. Who would have thought the writer would try to make good on his threat within the hour?

He should have, Reid thought. When his cell rang again, he grabbed it.

"Piper just called me again," Duncan said. "Nell asked the officer who responded to the attempted hit-and-run complaint to stay until one of us gets there."

"Smart," Reid said.

"Yeah, but we should have been smarter. I had Piper put the officer on the line. He filled me in on what the eyewitnesses saw. They say the driver of the car accelerated as soon as Piper stepped into the street—as if he'd been waiting for her. He would have run her down if Nell hadn't tackled her and gotten her out of the way."

Reid heard a thread of panic in his brother's voice he'd never heard before. "The important thing is that Piper's alive and unharmed." But he was thinking of Nell, the little fairy-tale princess of a girl he'd done his best to protect that long-ago summer. The image of her tackling her sister didn't quite gel with that. Nor did it fit with the fragile-looking teenage girl he recalled standing beneath the stone arch as their parents had taken their wedding vows.

"I knew there was another shoe that had to drop," Duncan said. "I should have known something like this might happen. The facts are all there. It's just that the attacks on Adair and Piper occurred at the castle, and only after they'd each found one of the earrings."

Reid had reviewed the same things in his own mind, until it had become a continuous loop. He'd first suggested they come to his office to get them out of the neighborhood. But he should have—

"I knew Deanna Lewis was working with someone," Duncan continued. "I knew they were obsessed with getting their hands on the Stuart sapphires. I should have—"

Reid cut his brother off by saying, "If it makes you feel any better, I've been blaming myself for not going there right after you called about the letters." Not that he would have gotten there in time. But he'd be there now.

There was a beat of silence on the other end of the line. Then Duncan said, "You've been blaming yourself?"

"That's what I said." With one hand, Reid eased the car out of the traffic circle.

"Wait. I'm going to punch the record button on my phone. Would you mind repeating that?"

"You can always dream, bro. And if you even breathe a word of that little confession to Cam, I'll deny it. Then I'll have to beat you up."

"*You* can always dream, bro."

With the panic in Duncan's voice replaced by humor, some of Reid's tension eased. But traffic had slowed to a crawl. Two blocks ahead, he saw the revolving lights of a patrol car. "I'm within sight of the apartment. I'll update you soon."

Reid jammed his car into a No Standing zone, jumped out and ran down the sidewalk.

NELL TURNED THE flame on beneath the teakettle on Piper's stove. She preferred coffee, but the ritual of making tea had always soothed her nerves. It brought back memories of the times she'd talked through her problems while she'd watched her aunt Vi brewing a pot in Castle MacPherson. Nell had spent a lot of time in the sunny kitchen after her sisters had left for college.

Adair had been the first to leave. Nell and Piper had shared one more year before Piper had deserted her, too. Then for her last two years of high school, she'd been alone. Of course, she'd still had her aunt Vi. And her father had been there, tucked away in his rooms painting or teaching some art classes at nearby Huntleigh College. But there'd been no one to sneak out to the stone arch with in the middle of the night, no one to laugh with as they'd written down their hopes and goals and dreams on different-colored papers and buried them.

Spotting the teapot in Piper's kitchen, Nell lifted it off the shelf, then nearly dropped it because her hands were trembling. So far she'd been able to hide that little fact from her sister. Since Piper's clothes looked as if they'd wiped the street, she was showering and changing before Duncan arrived.

Thank heavens Nell's own navy suit was made of some kind of miracle fabric she could roll up into a ball, stuff into a duffel bag and then shake out wrinkle-free. It had been perfect for her lifestyle during the past year. All she'd had to do to repair the damage from their close encounter with that wannabe hit-and-run driver was to sponge off a few spots of dust with cold water.

If only all her problems were that easy to solve. Tea, she reminded herself, as she searched through the cupboards and finally located the box. When it slipped through her fingers and landed on the floor, she retrieved it and set it gingerly on the counter. Pressing her palms flat on the ledge, she took a deep, calming breath.

She had to settle down. Once the nice young officer had taken their statements and escorted them up the alley stairs to her sister's apartment above a Georgetown boutique, her knees had begun to feel very weak.

A perfectly normal reaction, she'd told herself.

Someone was threatening her family. She hadn't heeded the warning in that first letter fast enough, and they'd taken action, nearly succeeding in killing Piper. Now that the initial adrenaline rush had worn off, shaking hands and wobbly knees were understandable.

But the butterflies in her stomach weren't just due to what had nearly happened in the street. They'd started frantically flapping their wings when Piper had told her that Reid Sutherland was on his way over. He would arrive momentarily.

Nell thought she'd have more time to prepare for meeting him again, time to think and to map out possible scenarios. Find the necklace first. Then deal with Reid Sutherland. Closing her eyes, she drew in another breath. The way she saw it, her problem was twofold. If he came to the castle with her, he posed a threat to her plan to prove to her family that she could take care of herself. The other problem was more personal. She wanted very much to bring to life her fantasies about seducing Reid. They couldn't be denied. Wouldn't be denied. But the last thing she needed to deal with right now was her attraction to him. She needed to find that necklace.

On her own.

Reid might present a challenge there, too. The Reid

she remembered had made all her decisions for her. And she'd let him.

She couldn't allow that to happen again. No way was she going to slip into her old habit of letting others involve themselves in her life and control it.

The sudden shriek of the teakettle made her jump. But it also jarred a thought loose. In a well-plotted story, the heroine never has the luxury of time to plan everything out.

She had to face the unexpected—and improvise. That was the key to a good page-turner.

It was also the key to becoming the truly independent woman she wanted to be. A girl would want to separate the two problems and solve them one at a time. A woman would take on the challenge of juggling two or three agendas.

Anyway, why not? A thrill moved through her just thinking about it. There had to be a way to find the necklace and fulfill that fantasy she'd written seven years ago. She'd just have to find it.

Turning off the kettle, she refocused her attention on making tea and noted with some satisfaction that her hands were steadier as she poured water into the china pot. Though the specific details of the sexual narratives she'd buried seven years ago remained a bit fuzzy, her overall goal was still crystal clear. That one searing look Reid had given her ages ago had awakened a desire in her that couldn't be denied. Wouldn't be denied.

All she had to do was find a way to convince him. She measured out tea leaves into a tea ball. As she swirled some of the hot water in the teapot to warm it first, then tipped out the water into the sink, she noted that her hands were perfectly steady.

Good. But this was *not* the time to wonder how it might feel when she ran them over Reid Sutherland's skin. After carefully adding boiling water to the china pot then adding the tea ball, she turned back to face the table. She had a much more pressing problem.

Someone had tried to run Piper down with a car.

Before her sister had gone into the bedroom to change, Nell had spread out all three letters carefully on the table so that when Duncan and Reid arrived, they could examine the evidence. The third letter frightened her the most.

Losing another member of your family.

The man who'd gunned his car straight at Piper wasn't fooling around.

Neither was she. Nell welcomed the spurt of anger. She turned back to the counter, opened a drawer, and located a pad of paper and a pen. From the time she'd first learned to write words, she'd made it a habit to capture her ideas on paper. Moving to the table, she read the third letter again.

This time it was something else entirely that jumped out at her.

Forty-eight hours.

That was the important part of the message. Why hadn't she absorbed it sooner? A ticking clock was a literary device many writers and moviemakers used. She wrote the number on the pad. The writer of this story wanted to put pressure on her to find the necklace fast.

The sudden knock at the door had her nearly dropping her pen.

"Duncan made good time," Piper called from the bedroom. "I'll be right out."

Nell set down her pad and pen on the counter, before

she moved to the door and opened it. It wasn't Duncan standing there. It was Reid. For the first time in her life, she experienced what it was like to be struck dumb. She couldn't breathe, couldn't move. Lucky for her, his attention was focused on the young officer who'd agreed to stand guard outside on the landing.

Hers was focused on Reid. She might have been transported back in time. Except he wasn't the same. On that day, her eyes had been riveted on a twenty-two-year-old boy on the edge of manhood. Right now she was looking at a man. Perhaps the most intimidating man that she'd ever seen. His shoulders were broader, his face leaner, the angles more defined. Even the long rangy body was more muscled.

Harder. That's what it was, she decided. Reid Sutherland looked bigger and harder than she had remembered him being. He was definitely not storybook prince material anymore. Those characters were never scary. And Reid was—just a little. When he turned, and she met his gaze, she realized that one thing was exactly the same. He could still make her throat go dry, make her bones melt in that strange way, and she had to press a hand to her heart when it gave that little flutter.

"Nell?"

She realized that she wasn't going to get his name past the dryness in her throat.

"Reid, come in." Piper joined her at the door. "The letters are on the table. Duncan?"

"On his way."

As Nell stepped aside and let Piper lead Reid into the kitchen, she felt a rush of relief. Her legs were working. He was standing in the tiny kitchen shrugging out of his suit jacket. Just to make sure she could, she shifted her gaze to Piper. Then she thanked the young officer who'd allowed Reid up the stairs.

No worries. Her body was working again. Any moment now her brain would catch up. It was all going to be good. She turned back to the kitchen. Reid stood in profile, leaning over the table reading the letters. He looked every bit as attractive and dangerous from the side as he had face-to-face. Her gaze went to the gun that he wore in a shoulder holster.

Of course he wore a gun. And of course he looked dangerous and intimidating. That was his job. What surprised her was she found the whole package incredibly arousing. She was just going to have to get used to the dry throat, the heat pooling in her center and the fluttering sensation beneath her heart.

Focus.

Following the direction of Reid's gaze, she looked at the three threatening notes on the table. They were what she had to concentrate on now.

HALF AN HOUR later, Reid leaned a hip against the counter in the tiny kitchen. The table offered two seats and as soon as his brother had arrived, Reid had encouraged Piper and Duncan to sit. Both of them were shaken up. Not surprising since two attempts had now been made on Piper's life in the past ten days.

Duncan was currently on the phone with a friend of his, Detective Mike Nelson, who was officially handling the case. One of his officers had already placed the three letters in evidence bags and taken them away. Reid was sure there wouldn't be any prints, other than Piper's and Nell's. Whoever had orchestrated the one-two-punch attack on the MacPherson sisters today had planned it too carefully to make a careless mistake. According to the young officer on the landing, the second part of the punch had come within a hairbreadth of being successful. The bastard would have run Piper down on the street if not for Nell's quick thinking and amazing reflexes.

Reid shifted his gaze to where she stood arranging mugs on a tray and once more absorbed the overload to his senses. He was almost getting used to her effect on him.

Almost.

He certainly hadn't been prepared when she'd opened the door of the apartment. That first sight of her had hit him in the gut with the power a double-barreled shotgun. The sexual pull had been even more potent and primitive than he'd recalled. Seven years ago, he could blame it on hormones, but he found it harder to rationalize it now and impossible to deny.

Thinking back, he recalled that he'd sensed her the instant she'd opened the door—a tingling awareness along all of his nerve endings. And he'd caught her scent—something he couldn't quite describe. When he had turned away from the young officer and looked into her eyes, his mind had gone clear as glass, and all he'd seen was her.

All of her.

He was trained to take in numerous details in one glance, but they'd never registered so clearly on his senses before that he'd lost track of his surroundings. In that freeze-framed instant in time, he was completely absorbed in taking her in. The golden-blond hair that was clipped back from her face fell below her shoulders. The jacket and pants in some clingy fabric revealed a neat athletic body with more curves and longer legs than he remembered. Even as he registered all of that, his gaze hadn't wavered from her face. He couldn't look away from those eyes. They were still that dark, deep blue—the color of Eleanor's sapphires—and every bit as fascinating. Then there was the pale-as-milk skin, the soft unpainted mouth, the lips that were slightly parted. In surprise? Anticipation?

Nell? There was a question in the word he'd spoken, but he still wasn't sure what he'd been asking. What he knew was that for an instant he'd been tempted to step forward and take a taste of that mouth. It was fear that had kept him from moving. Fear that he might not be able to stop with a kiss.

No woman had ever made him afraid before.

Then Piper had come to the door, and he'd remembered who he was, where he was, and that this was Nell.

His stepsister.

He wished he could think of her only that way—the tiny and fragile girl who had to be cared for and protected. But the girl he'd carried around in his memory was turning out to be a sharp right turn from the woman who'd rescued her sister with a flying tackle. As a man who had fine-tuned his abilities to anticipate the future, Reid normally didn't like surprises. But in Nell's case, there was a part of him that was looking forward to them.

As long as they didn't distract him from the job he had to do. The MacPherson sisters were currently the priority he had to focus on.

He shifted his gaze back to the table where Piper was frowning down at her cell phone, examining the photos she'd taken of the three letters as if she had missed something. But she hadn't missed anything. The message was clear. Someone, and he was betting it was Deanna Lewis's partner, wanted Eleanor's sapphires badly enough to kill off the remaining members of the MacPherson family to get them. The would-be killer's focus seemed to be on the sisters for now, but the threats extended to their father, his mother, their aunt Vi. And because of their relationship with Adair and Piper, Cam and Duncan could also be on the list.

"Send me something as soon as you have it," Duncan said, then ended his call. "Nelson says that the car was just reported stolen from a hotel parking garage. But two of the eyewitnesses have arrived at the precinct. They're going to work with a sketch artist. If all goes well, they'll have something to put on the early-evening news."

"The sketch probably won't help us much," Nell said as she served tea to Piper and Duncan. "Both witnesses said the driver was wearing a hat low on his forehead, a beard and sunglasses. Those are pretty standard items for a disguise. In fact, he could even be a she."

Reid exchanged a glance with his brother. He was impressed with her analysis. And her focus. It was stronger than his was.

Piper frowned at her cell. "You should have told us the second you received the first letter."

Nell moved forward and rested a hand on Piper's shoulder. "I should have acted faster after I received the first letter. I won't make that mistake again. Whoever is behind the notes planned everything very carefully, and I must have been under surveillance. In Louisville, the letter was delivered to my work. To do that here in D.C., the job was trickier. The manager of Pages told me the sign's been in the window for almost a month, so the author of the letter knew exactly when I'd be there to sign for it. Arranging for the instant delivery was a piece of cake. But he had only a few hours to verify that Piper was with me and that we'd eventually have to cross the street to get to the apartment. It was a good bet that we'd stop for lunch or coffee at the café. We've done that every day since I arrived. All he had to do was wait."

"I agree," Duncan said. "He planned everything meticulously."

High praise from a profiler, Reid thought.

"But here's the thing," Nell said. "He couldn't have possibly known that Piper would step into the street alone. We could have been together just as easily."

As she described what had happened just before the attempted hit-and-run, Reid pictured it in his mind—something he should have been doing much earlier. "Why weren't you in the street with her?"

"She left fast," Nell said.

"And Nell always moves slow," Piper added.

"Wait. I remember now," Nell said. "There was a woman who came up to me and asked me for an autograph."

"I didn't see that," Piper said.

"You were talking to your boss on your cell. The woman said she'd missed the signing, and she wanted me to sign a copy of my book for her daughter. Then I was distracted by that horn again, and I heard the motor racing. I just pushed past her."

Reid reached for his jacket. "C'mon. Let's go down to the street and walk through it."

5

THE STREET IN front of Piper's apartment had returned to normal. Tourists and shoppers strolled along the sidewalks, some stopping to peer in windows. Nell noted that both Duncan and Reid were in full bodyguard mode, walking on the outside as they escorted the sisters across the street and along the sidewalk to the café.

They stopped just in front of the table where she and Piper had sat earlier. Reid made sure that she was just a bit behind him and to his left. That way he could shove her out of the way with his left hand and draw his gun with his right. Perfect, Nell thought. She had to stifle the urge to stop and make a note of it on her pad.

"Tell us what happened, Nell," Reid said, "just as if you were writing it. And we'll act it out."

Nell pointed to the street. "Piper, you were right there."

As Duncan and Piper moved into position between two parked cars, she said, "I heard the horn first and I glanced down the street to see this car holding up traffic. He was double-parked in front of the art store, and the driver behind him was getting impatient. I was about to join Piper when the woman came up to me with the book."

"And you signed it?" Reid asked.

Nell shook her head. "No. I was reaching for it when the horn distracted me again. Then everything happened at once. I heard the motor, saw the blur of motion, and I just ran toward Piper."

Reid took her arm and drew her with him toward the art store. When they reached it, he glanced up and back down the street. Then he signaled Piper and Duncan to join them.

"Nell says the car was stopped here blocking other cars when she first spotted it," he explained. "But he couldn't have been here long. Too much traffic."

"I bet he was illegally standing in that loading zone two stores down," Nell said. He could have idled there until Piper stood up. Then he pulled out into traffic and waited. That's the way I would have written it."

Reid glanced at her. "You could be right."

Nell heard something in his tone that she'd never heard before. Surprise? Admiration? Whatever it was, it sent a little stream of warmth through her.

"I'm sure she's right," Duncan said. "The guy's been watching her every movement since she arrived in town. He was watching her in Louisville, too."

"I'll bet the loading zone offers a good view of the café," Nell said.

When they reached the empty space two stores down and stepped into the street, Nell continued. "From here, he could see Piper drop the money on the table."

"Then I just walked away," Piper said. "I was totally focused on calling my boss to tell him I'd be late. Family emergency."

Reid could picture it very clearly in his mind—the driver pulling out and blocking the traffic. He should have seen it before. The problem was that his brain had been working in slow motion ever since he'd looked into Nell's eyes again. He had to change that—and fast.

"I'm about to join her when the woman comes up to me with the book," Nell said. "If it weren't for a driver who was heavy-handed with his horn, I wouldn't have turned to look. He would have had a clear shot to hit Piper."

"Gutsy bastard," Reid murmured. He pictured the acceleration, the collision. He frowned. "He wouldn't have been able to build up much speed. He couldn't have been certain he'd kill her."

"He didn't have to. All he had to do was make me think he *could* kill her."

They all turned to stare at her.

"He clearly intended to hit her. She could have been killed," Duncan pointed out.

"But hit-and-run is sloppy," Nell said. "Especially in Georgetown traffic. I think his real goal is to make me *believe* he's ready to pick off my family one member at a time so that I'll find the sapphire necklace for him and hand it over. Which is what I'm going to do."

"I don't think he's quite as nice a guy as you're imagining him to be," Reid said. "My guess is that he had murder on his mind, but he wasn't a professional."

"If he's anything like Deanna Lewis, he's not nice at all," Piper said. "Nell, it's too dangerous for you to go to the castle. You'll stay here with me, and we'll get protection. It's going to be all right."

Nell took her sister's hands. "You've been telling me that all my life. Now it's my turn to tell you this. I'm going to fix this. He's given me forty-eight hours. The clock is ticking. It's the oldest plot device in the world. But it works. So I'm going to the castle, and I'm going to find Eleanor's necklace. He'll follow me up there, because the Stuart sapphires are what he really wants."

Piper looked from Duncan to Reid and back to Duncan again. "One of you has to talk some sense into her."

Reid glanced at his brother, then said, "The thing is, she's making sense. At the very least, she has to go to the castle and go through the motions of looking for the necklace. That will buy us forty-eight hours to put an end to this. I'm going with her."

"In the meantime, we'll beef up protection for the whole family," Duncan added.

"IT'S GOING TO be all right," Nell said as she checked her suitcase for the last time. She was beginning to really enjoy saying those words to her sister. What she wasn't enjoying was the fact that Piper was so worried. Though there wasn't much space in the small bedroom, Piper was pacing just as she always had when something was really bothering her.

Nell glanced into the bathroom, checked the shelves one last time. The rest of her family would worry also. Duncan and Reid were filling them in on the plan right now. At least Aunt Vi wasn't alone at the castle. Daryl Garnett, her fiancé, who headed up the domestic division of the CIA, was with her. He'd taken some time off when Adair and Cam had left for Scotland to help Vi run the wedding business and make sure she was safe.

Piper stopped her pacing, sat on the foot of the bed and patted the space next to her. When Nell joined her, Piper said, "I just wish I could go with you."

"Your big trial starts on Monday. You need to be here. You'll be safer here."

"So will you. There are so many ways to sneak onto the castle grounds. And there's a wedding scheduled there on Saturday. A rehearsal tomorrow. Those will provide ample opportunity for someone to get close to you."

"I'll have two agents watching over me. And I'll know that Duncan will keep you safe."

Piper frowned at her. "Only because you're drawing this person away. You're making a target out of yourself."

"I'm also making a target out of Reid. I can't believe whoever this is will be happy that I'm taking a Secret Service agent with me. Deanna's partner will follow me to the castle, and I think he'll keep a close eye on me."

"You're not making me feel better," Piper said.

"I'm just thinking of their side of the story. Clearly they believe they have a right to those jewels, and if they turn out to be descendants of the Stuarts, they could be right."

"But we're Eleanor's descendants," Piper said.

"Exactly." Nell beamed a smile at her. "It will all boil down to a classic case of conflicting narratives. You deal with that in court every day. The thing is, they may have a more powerful claim on the jewels. Yet we've always believed that they were Eleanor's dowry."

"Well, the jury's out on that one."

"Agreed," Nell said. "But wouldn't the possibility make you just keep turning the pages to find out?"

Piper stared at her sister. "This isn't some story you're writing, Nell."

"No." But it was certainly a story she was thinking

of writing. The twist would fit well in the book she was working on—an adult thriller with a romantic subplot.

There was a knock on the bedroom door and Duncan said, "You two ready in there?"

"Yes." Piper rose and took Nell's suitcase. "The only reason I'm letting you go is because Reid's going with you. No one could be more devoted to protecting you than he is."

True, Nell thought. Yet having a guardian angel along was going to make it difficult to find the necklace on her own without being protected by Reid. But that wasn't her only problem. Difficulty number two was she wasn't sure she wanted to be protected *from* Reid.

But that was an entirely different story line, one she wasn't quite ready to share with her sister. She had to plot it out for herself first.

AN HOUR LATER, Reid found himself folded up like an accordion in the front seat of Nell's sporty little Fiat as she shot it up a ramp onto the beltway that would take them out of D.C. Using the side-view mirror, he checked the cars behind them.

"You think he'll try to follow us?" Nell asked.

"It's a good possibility," he said. "He'll want to make sure you're headed up to the castle."

"That's what your work is like, isn't it? Coming up with all the possibilities?"

"Yes."

"Writers have to do that, too. Except that we can choose one of the possibilities, and you have to deal with what you get. Like getting stuck with me and going up to the castle."

"I wouldn't call that getting stuck." But he was definitely stuck big-time in her little car.

The seat was pushed back as far as it would go, but he still felt as if he'd been stuffed into a shoe box. And he was listening to Bach or Beethoven or Brahms on the radio. He'd never been able to keep those classical composers straight.

He had no one to blame but himself for the cramped conditions. Nell had made several arguments while they'd taken the short walk to where he'd illegally parked his sedan. That was something she hadn't done when she was six. That summer she'd been willing and eager to do everything he told her.

First she'd demanded they take two cars. In separate vehicles, it would be less obvious that she'd acquired a bodyguard. He'd countered by pointing out that, once they got to the castle, his presence would be clear to anyone. Then she'd gone for the emotional appeal—she'd feel more comfortable if she had her own vehicle. After all, it had been the only steady companion she'd had for the past year when she'd toured the country teaching classes and promoting her book.

But if there was one thing he'd picked up on in the past two hours, it was that Nell was most interested in being a key player in recovering Eleanor's necklace. Bottom line—she wanted her own car, because it would give her a certain amount of independence. It was that desire to operate independently that was going to make his job more challenging. His knees were bumping against the dashboard right now because he intended to indulge her need for independence on the less important issues so that he could successfully block it on the more important ones.

That had always been his strategy with the VP. Nell was going into a dangerous situation at the castle. She'd put on a cheery act for her sister, and she might have an overly optimistic view on how everything was going to work out, but he didn't doubt for a moment that she had a clear outlook on the situation.

This couldn't be easy for her. One minute she'd been signing her books and looking forward to spending another few days with her sister. The next, someone had tried to run down Piper, immediately followed by another written threat against her family.

"We're going to find a way through this, Nell."

"I know."

The confidence in her tone had him looking at her. It occurred to him for the first time that her attitude might be fueled by more than her overly optimistic nature. "Do you have some idea about where the necklace is?"

"No." She shifted to the center lane as traffic began to clog the right lane. "But I've been thinking about it ever since Adair found the first earring. There's got to be a story behind the way Eleanor divided them up and hid them in different places."

"You think she had a method to her madness?" he asked.

"Exactly. With characters, motivation is always key. One of Eleanor's reasons for hiding the jewels had to be that she didn't want to pass them on to members of her own family. That has to be why she didn't hide them inside the castle. I think that once it was discovered that they were missing, the surviving children must have searched every inch of that place."

"Yet Cam believes that whoever is behind this believed that either she hid the sapphires or some kind of clue in the library."

"That's a very logical theory," Nell conceded. "If I were Eleanor, I'd want to leave behind something to point the way. Yet my sisters came upon the earrings without any clue at all."

Reid shifted to study her a moment. "Do you have a theory about that?"

"It's more of a story idea."

"Tell me."

She shot him a quick look. "Promise you won't laugh."

Intrigued now, he said, "I won't. Cross my heart."

"That's what you always used to say to me whenever I got scared that summer we played together. All those days when it was your job to get me up to the cave in the cliff face so that I could wait around to be rescued, you'd say, "You'll be safe, Nell. Cross my heart. Remember?'"

Reid could hardly forget. Hands down, his brothers' favorite game that summer had been pirates hunting for treasure—the treasure being Eleanor's sapphires. Of course, any pirate had to kidnap and hold a fair damsel captive. After the first game, it had been Reid's idea that Nell should have the permanent role of kidnapped damsel. It had been the only way to keep her off the cliff face and safe. "I never lied. And you're stalling. Tell me your story idea."

She passed a truck, shifted back into the right lane and said, "Okay. First, Eleanor wanted to leave proof behind that the jewels existed and had been in her possession. That's why she wore them in the portrait. And she wanted the sapphires to eventually be discovered. She didn't just throw them away. The two earrings were very carefully wrapped in leather pouches and hidden in places built to survive time and weather. So far the jewels have been found in the places we played as children—in the stone arch and the cave."

"Correct."

"So—and this is the 'don't laugh part.' She hid each piece separately—so maybe she wanted them to be found now, and by my sisters and me."

"You're implying that she had some insight into the future."

"Something like that."

For a moment, Reid considered. "That idea might work very well for a children's story."

"But it's not a possibility that a Secret Service agent would entertain."

"No. We work in much more concrete scenarios."

"Hypothetical or concrete, we're both after the same thing," Nell said, easing the car into the center lane again.

"With one important difference. You want to discover the story about the sapphires, why Eleanor hid them, figure out who they belong to and why someone else believes they have a claim on them. My goal is much simpler. I want to catch a would-be killer and write 'the end' on the story."

She shot him a grin. "Works for me. And thanks for not laughing." Then she turned her full attention back to negotiating her way through traffic.

By the time they'd cleared the D.C. area and had entered Pennsylvania, Reid became aware that he had a bigger problem than the cramp in his leg. He'd been trained to use all of his senses, and sitting in the tiny space with Nell, he'd found that he was definitely using all of them.

First, there was no escaping her scent. He still hadn't come up with a description. But he'd smelled it before, perhaps in the gardens at the White House at night. He'd kept his eyes on the road, but he had excellent peripheral vision, and he'd been trained to use it. Therefore, in the space of thirty miles, he'd become very aware of the soft curve of her lips when she smiled, and that the sun lightened the color of her hair. He'd also had time to study her hands. They were small, the fingers slender. She wore her nails short with just a sheen of pink polish. A lady's hands. And twice so far, he'd caught himself imagining what they might feel like on his skin. He'd found out when they'd both reached to turn the radio station at the same time. Her fingers had just brushed lightly against the back of his hand, but the burning sensation had shot right to his loins.

"Sorry." They'd both spoken at once.

She'd laughed and held up one hand with her little finger extended. "Pinkie wish."

"Pinkie what?"

"We both said the same word at the same time. Now we're supposed to link our little fingers and make a wish. C'mon."

"Okay." He linked his pinkie finger with hers and felt the arrow of heat shoot through him again.

It gave him some satisfaction that her hand trembled just a little as she placed it back on the wheel. But he shouldn't be hoping she might be feeling even some part of the attraction he was feeling. Because he shouldn't be feeling this way; he shouldn't be wanting Nell MacPherson.

The problem was, like it or not, he did. And the desire to have her was growing with each passing mile.

"Well, are you going to do something about it or should I?" Nell asked him.

Everything in his body went hard as he turned to stare at her. "Do something about what?"

"The static on the radio. What did you think I was talking about?"

Not going there, Reid thought. "What do you like?" But even that question had his mind wandering beyond her taste in music. How did she like to be touched? Tasted?

"I have pretty eclectic tastes."

Good to know.

"But Piper's been listening to that classic station for three days now. I need a change. Do you like the Beatles?"

"Who doesn't?"

This time he kept his hands to himself as she punched some buttons and "I Want to Hold Your Hand" blasted into the small car. Listening to it didn't solve his problem. He wanted to do a lot more than hold Nell's hand.

She lowered the volume. He tried to do the same with the desire that was thrumming through him. He had only briefly touched the woman, not yet kissed her on the lips. His hormones hadn't run this hot since he was in college.

Not since the last time he'd seen Nell beneath the stone arch.

Grimly, Reid shifted his attention to the side view mirror again and watched that for a while. "Pass a few cars," he said.

While she did, he kept his gaze fixed. He saw what he was looking for when the highway began to climb.

"There's been a silvery-gray sedan three cars back for a while now," she said.

Surprised, he shot her a sideways glance. "You noticed it."

"You said it was possible he'd follow us, so I thought it might be a good idea to keep a lookout. That car was behind us when we drove onto the beltway. It got ahead of us about twenty miles back, but we passed it when traffic got congested again before the last exit."

The woman had good eyes. He, too, had noted the cars that had followed them onto the interstate, but he'd lost track of the gray sedan after it had passed them.

Because he'd been thinking of Nell.

A sign for the upcoming exit flashed by. "Cut back into the right-hand lane and take your speed down to just below the limit."

Nell did exactly as he asked. Within minutes, the car directly behind them cut into the passing lane and drove by. The gray sedan merely slowed and kept its distance. Before long, several more cars passed.

"What now?" Nell asked.

"A break," he announced. "We're going to take the next exit ramp and stop for some coffee, stretch our legs and see if the gray car follows us."

A break sounded like a very good idea. The fast-food chain they stopped at had a drive-through, so Nell was surprised when Reid told her to park. The gray car not only followed them onto the exit ramp, it turned into the restaurant behind them. By the time Nell eased her Fiat into the parking slot and turned off the engine, the gray car was moving past them toward the drive-through lane. Nell caught a glimpse of the driver in her rearview mirror and gasped.

"What?" Reid asked.

"The driver of the car that's been following us. It's the woman who came up to me in the café and asked me to autograph that book. I'm sure of it."

6

REID TURNED TO face Nell and blocked her view of the car. "Don't look at her again and stay right where you are. I'm going to get out and come around to your door."

Nell's mind raced almost as fast as her heart while Reid took his time extricating himself from the front seat and circling the front of the car. She summoned up the image of the woman who'd approached her on the sidewalk and compared it to the quick glimpse she'd gotten of the driver. The same hair, the glint of gold at her ear. It was her all right. Though Nell badly wanted to, she didn't look at the gray car again. Another vehicle drove past. In the rearview mirror she could see it was a big SUV with at least half a Little League baseball team packed into it. In her peripheral vision, she saw it follow the gray car into the drive-through lane.

Then Reid opened her door and extended his hand to help her out. When it closed over hers, the effect on her system was instantaneous. She stilled in her seat. All thought of the autograph lady faded from her mind as it filled with Reid. Just the sight of her hand lost in his had all of her senses heightening. She noticed the contrasts first. His hand was larger, broader, and his skin made hers look even paler. His palms were hard. She felt the pressure of each one of his fingers as they tensed on hers. There was power there. Danger. It pulled at her in a way nothing else ever had. Her body heated so quickly the hot afternoon sun felt cool on her skin. When she looked up to meet his eyes, she saw the same intensity that she felt in the grip of his hand. The gray of his irises had darkened. His hand tightened on hers and for a moment she thought he would help her up and then right into his arms.

She had to find out. Her mind was already racing forward, anticipating what would happen when her body was pressed fully to his, what she would feel when his mouth closed over hers.

Before she could move, he stepped back and shifted his gaze over the top of the car. Then he dropped her hand and closed the door. She made some kind of sound, but he was already moving around the front of the car. Biting down hard on her lip, Nell desperately tried to gather her wits. The time it took for him to insert himself into the front seat again helped. A little. But her heart pounded so hard and so fast she could hardly hear him when he finally spoke.

"She's gone around the corner, and she's trapped by the two cars that pulled in behind her. She's probably expecting us to go in."

His words and the brusque tone helped her to focus on reality. And on the woman who'd followed them from D.C. A woman who had played a role in nearly killing her sister.

Gripping the steering wheel, she forced herself to relive that horrifying moment when she was racing toward Piper, hoping and praying that she'd get to her before that car did. That did the trick. What she was feeling about Reid and what she wanted to do about it had to be shoved to the back burner for now. They had bigger and much more dangerous fish to fry.

"She can't afford to stay too close or to follow us into the restaurant. She has to be careful I don't recognize her," she said.

"Good point," Reid acknowledged.

"Still she's taking a risk. We could leave right now and be out of sight by the time she gets through the drive-through. But there may be another reason why she can afford to let us out of her sight for a few minutes."

"What are you thinking?"

Nell turned to face him. "She might not be our only tail. And you're thinking that, too. Aren't you? That's why we're still sitting here instead of going into the restaurant, isn't it?"

Surprise flickered in his eyes. "That's exactly what I'm thinking."

"I should have thought of it sooner," she said.

"Why would you?"

"Because one of my guilty pleasures is watching TV shows about crime fighters. I'm addicted to this one about this ex-CIA agent who's been burned from his job and is working for private clients in Miami. He and his pals use the double-tail strategy all the time. Police use it, too."

"So does the Secret Service," Reid said in a dry tone. "Let's put your theory to the test. If I'd set up the double tail, the second car would have pulled to the shoulder on the interstate and will be waiting to pick us up when we return. Back out and use the entrance to get us out of here."

Nell started the car, shot it into Reverse, then drove out the same way they'd come in. Turning left, she headed back toward the interstate. Three cars were waiting in a line to make a turn onto the highway. Other than that, there was no traffic, and no one had followed them out of the restaurant. "We're clear."

When she put on her signal to turn onto the interstate ramp, Reid said, "Keep going. You have a GPS system in the car, right?"

She glanced at him as she reached for the button to activate it. "What's the plan?"

"My guess is that the second tail is waiting for us near the entrance ramp, and your autograph hound won't panic until she picks up her drive-through order and notices that our car is gone. Her first call will be to the second tail. Keep your eye on the restaurant in your rearview mirror, while I find us a back-road route to Albany."

"Albany?" It was her turn to feel surprised.

Reid's fingers were busy on the console. "Just as soon as we're sure no one is following us, we're going to use an hour of the forty-four or so we have left to pay a visit to Deanna Lewis."

"She's still in a coma."

He pushed a button. "True. But I'd like to see her in person and talk to the staff. If we'd stayed on the interstate, we would have had to drive around Albany. This way our tail or tails won't know about our visit. Any sign of the gray car yet?"

She checked the rearview mirror. "No. And the three

cars exiting from the toll area all headed in the direction of the restaurant. We're still clear."

"Turn left at that intersection ahead."

Once she made the turn, Reid pulled out his cell. "Keep your eye out. I'm going to text gray car's license plate to Duncan." After a moment, he continued, "Can you describe the woman who asked you for the autograph?"

"Sure." After glancing in the rearview mirror again, Nell pictured in her mind the woman who'd come up to her in the café. "Long dark hair pulled back from her face with a gold clip. Not pretty, but very attractive. Early to mid-fifties, but she takes some care to look younger. Makeup, manicure and expensive clothes. She was wearing a silk shirt, gold necklace and earrings. And a ring on her left hand with some kind of insignia. Maybe a coat of arms."

She felt Reid glance up from his cell phone to look at her for a moment.

"Do you look at everyone you meet that closely?"

"I suppose," she said. "I never know when I might need those details for a character I'm writing."

"Did you notice anything else?"

"She spoke with a slight accent. British perhaps."

For the next fifteen minutes, there was silence in the car except for the low throbbing beat of the Beatles retrospective on the radio. With the road stretching out before her like an endless ribbon, Nell found her mind arrowing back to those few world-stopping moments in the parking lot when Reid had grasped her hand to pull her out of the car.

Earlier, when they'd made that pinkie wish, she'd nearly convinced herself that he hadn't shared that hot explosion of desire that she'd experienced. But during that space of time when she'd been anticipating the kiss she'd fantasized about for years, she hadn't been mistaken about his response. His intention. She couldn't have felt what she had if he had felt nothing. She'd taken enough chemistry in school to know the basics. Two substances had to interact for combustion to take place.

Just thinking about what might have happened if he'd kissed her triggered flames that licked along her nerve endings.

Breathe. She could barely feel her fingers on the steering wheel.

Focus. After checking the mirror again, Nell allowed herself a sideways glance at Reid. He was texting back and forth with Duncan. Doing what needed to be done. And what she needed to do was drive to Albany. But sooner or later, they were going to have to talk about what was going on between them and what they were going to do about it.

Just the thought of "doing something" was enough to release the floodgates again. She felt the torrid liquid heat flowing through her system, enough to make her shiver.

"You okay?" Reid asked.

It's all good, she told herself. "I'm fine," she said.

On second thought, perhaps it was best that they didn't talk about what was happening between them at all and just get to the *doing it* part. At any rate, now wasn't the time or the place. There were much better settings.

Once more, she checked the mirror. No sign of a gray car or any other vehicle. A glance at the GPS screen on her console told her that they were still ten miles from the outskirts of Albany. With nothing but a constantly unrolling ribbon of road in front of her, Nell increased the pressure on the gas pedal and thought of where at the castle she and Reid might have their "talk." Or not.

In the little fantasy she wrote about Reid all those years ago and buried in the metal box, the setting she'd chosen was in the gardens. She had to avoid the stone arch. Because the fantasies she'd spun about him had nothing to do with happy-ever-afters and everything to do with slow, teasing arousal and hot, unbridled chemistry.

Or at least, that's what she'd known about those things at eighteen. The gardens had always been her favorite on the castle grounds. There was one particular spot that had been her secret place—one she'd escaped to when she wanted to get away from her sisters and even Aunt Vi. She'd even plotted out the first draft of *It's All Good* there.

Little wonder her favorite place had come to mind when she'd written down her most secret and sexy narrative. There'd be moonlight, of course. A full moon over the lake and lots of stars. And the heady scent of flowers, some of which had been planted by Eleanor herself.

With the image fully delineated in her mind, she risked a quick glance at Reid. In her current reality, he was fully dressed in his Secret Service suit, all neat and tidy except for the loosened tie. He wouldn't need all those clothes in the garden. Not any of them, if her story line went according to plan.

She pictured taking his shirt off, exposing that tanned skin an inch at a time. The moonlight would play over it as she ran her hand over his shoulders, testing the smooth, firm flesh and the hard muscle beneath. Then she'd draw the shirt slowly down his arms until it hung from his wrists, trapping them. Yes, that would be good, she thought. He wouldn't be able to touch her as she began to explore his flesh with her mouth.

Nell? That would be the only word he'd say. The same way he'd said it when he had first seen her in Piper's apartment. It would have the same question in the tone. And this time she'd have the answer.

"Nell, are you all right?"

She tensed her fingers on the wheel and jerked herself back to her current reality. Then she slammed on the brakes to avoid running the red light ahead of her. "I'm fine."

"You seemed to be a thousand miles away."

Less than fifty, if she was judging the distance to the castle gardens correctly. "Just thinking."

"Here's more to think about. Duncan had some luck running the plates. The gray car is registered to a Gwendolen Campbell. And she spells it the same way one of Eleanor Campbell's older sisters did." Reid filled her in on the family lineage Cam had told him about that morning.

"What are the chances that two hundred years later we'd be tailed by someone who just happens to have the same name as Eleanor Campbell's sister? Right down to the spelling?"

"Duncan's going to do what he can to check her out. In the meantime, he's filling Cam in on the latest, and one of them will inform Daryl Garnett, so he's fully briefed when we arrive at the castle."

As the light turned, Reid noticed that the road had widened into four lanes. They were still on the outskirts of Albany, but he could see the capital buildings in the distance to his left, and the traffic had grown heavier. To his right he noted a sign that they were approaching a hospital.

"Well, with the CIA on our team both here and in Scotland, we ought to know more soon," Nell said. "In the meantime, we know that Gwendolen Campbell is definitely involved in this. The question is, how involved? Who is she working with besides Deanna Lewis and the man or woman who tried to run Piper down? And who's running the show?"

He shot Nell a sideways glance. He couldn't have put it better himself. Her questions were spot-on. "I should have seen she had to be a player when you first mentioned your autograph lady. Maybe the key player. More than that, we've been assuming that the *us* Deanna Lewis was talking about to Piper involved just two people, that Deanna had one partner. There could be three. But there could be more. That possibility should have occurred to me sooner."

"Well, if you want to play the blame game, I should have figured it out, too." Nell changed into the right lane. "I make up plotlines. And her request for that autograph had perfect timing. Plus, she looked so normal. All I saw was a woman who wanted me to sign a book for her granddaughter. And that makes her perfect for the role of villain."

She took a right turn toward the hospital. "I should have seen it. I was just too focused on Piper after the attempt. I wouldn't have even thought about the woman again if you hadn't probed."

The difference was Nell had good reason for her distraction. Someone had tried to run down her sister. But

Reid had only one reason for his lapse. Nell. He'd been thinking about her and wanting her ever since he'd seen her again. He couldn't seem to get any distance or perspective. It wasn't just the sexual attraction—although it was there, a steady burn in his blood. A strong part of his distraction was due to the fact that she'd changed in very surprising ways. He was constantly being delighted and fascinated by the way her mind worked.

"Something's bothering you," Nell said.

Then there was her talent for intuiting things about him: the way he was feeling and what he was thinking. Not even his brothers could do that.

And if he kept wondering how *she* could or what she might do next to surprise him, he wasn't going to be able to protect her.

"No one's following us." She turned into the hospital parking lot. "This was a great idea. Our quick exit from the fast-food restaurant bought us some time. At the castle, Daryl Garnett is with Aunt Vi, and from what Piper and Adair say, Vi is in very good hands. So even if autograph lady or one of her partners gets annoyed that we've taken this detour, I think everyone should be safe for the moment."

"You're the one I'm worried about. You're distracting me from this investigation, and that puts you in danger."

Nell's heart gave a little flutter, but she managed to keep her hands steady on the wheel as she drove down the line of cars and pulled into a parking space. Saying a little prayer that her voice would work, she faced him. "I can take care of myself. If it makes you feel any better, you're distracting me, too."

Reid frowned. "That only makes the problem worse. We have to sort this out and find a solution."

Nell knew exactly how she wanted to solve their problem. The image flashed into her mind of the scene she'd created earlier—the two of them in Eleanor's moonlit garden. She could almost feel the smooth taut skin of his bare shoulders beneath her hands. Reminding herself to breathe, she said, "The clock is ticking. We should discuss this after we get to the castle."

"We'll settle it now, in just a second. Stay right where you are." Reid opened the car door and climbed out to scan the lot.

While he did his bodyguard thing, Nell remained seated, gathered her thoughts. So much for the little garden in the moonlight scene. In that particular setting, she hadn't planned on doing a lot of talking. None at all, in fact. But any heroine worth her salt could adapt to the changing circumstances. All she had to do was tell him what she wanted.

Him.

When he climbed back into the car, he seemed to fill every inch of space until he was all she was aware of. His eyes were the color of smoke shooting up from a fire, dark and dangerous. And his lips were so close. The air in the cramped space had turned sultry. Stifling. She couldn't tear her gaze away from his mouth. It seemed to be the softest part of him; still, it looked firm and unyielding. What would it feel like pressed against hers? Gentle? Rough? Another inch and their lips would make contact. How long had she yearned for the moment? All she had to do was lean forward and…

Hard hands gripped her shoulders, making it impossible for her to move.

"I want you, Nell. I can't seem to change that. But

one thing I can control. Nothing is going to happen between us."

She felt as if he'd upended a bucket of ice water on her head.

Wanna bet? If she could have moved her lips, she would have said it out loud. She might even have stuck out her tongue. Neither was her best move if she wanted Reid to start thinking of her as a woman. A woman he was incapable of resisting. She needed another strategy. Fast.

"Nothing," he repeated as if he could read her mind.

She recognized the steely determination in his tone, and it only added fuel to her own resolve. During that long-ago summer, he'd used that same tone to convince her that she could reach any goal, conquer any obstacle. She'd obeyed him like a slave, taken any risk he'd challenged her with. Those days were gone.

"Why not? We're both adults. We want each other. What could be the harm?"

For an instant his hands tightened on her shoulders, and she was sure he was going to pull her closer. He gave her a hard shake.

Then he dropped his hands clenching them into fists. "You're family. Dammit, Nell, I don't want to hurt you."

Nell's temper flared. "You know what your problem is, Reid? Like the rest of my family, you're making some very false assumptions." She poked a finger into his chest. "One, you believe I'm still a little girl, someone you have to take care of. You're wrong. I can take care of myself."

"Maybe. But you deserve someone who'll offer you more than I can. You deserve what your sisters have found with my brothers. You'll expect that. Everyone in the family will. I decided a long time ago that I wouldn't be able to offer any woman that."

She poked him again. "You're wrong about my expectations, too. The last thing in the world I want is some kind of permanent involvement with a man. I'm three years out of college. I have to concentrate on my career. Besides, I tried the whole falling-in-love thing a few years back, and it drained too much time out of my writing schedule, not to mention the effect it had on my GPA. Even if I was ready for something long-term, you'd be the last man I'd choose."

"Why?"

"Because you're overprotective just like the rest of my family. It's bad enough that I'm stuck working with you to find the necklace. I intended to do that on my own."

After a beat of silence, his eyes narrowed on her. He was listening now. "The man you fell in love with—he hurt you."

"Yes, but I got over it. I'm a big girl. You're going to have to get used to that."

Another beat of silence.

"Is there anything else I got wrong?"

"Yes. You're absolutely wrong when you say 'Nothing can happen between us' because something already has. Back in the parking lot of that restaurant, I wanted to kiss you. And you wanted it, too. We're both thinking about what it would be like. I'm imagining one thing. You're probably envisioning another. In one of my books, this would be a plot point. The characters would have to make a decision. Either they find out and deal with the consequences, or they keep thinking about it. I would assume that, in your job, it pays to know exactly what you're up against. Right?"

"Close enough."

But *he* wasn't nearly close enough. The heat of his breath burned her lips, but she had to have more. And talking wasn't going to get it for her. If she wanted to seduce Reid, *she* had to make the move.

Finally, her arms were around him, her mouth parted beneath his. And she had her answers.

His mouth wasn't soft at all but open and urgent. His taste was as dark and dangerous as the man. That much she'd guessed. But there was none of the control that he always seemed to coat himself with. None of the reserve. There was only heat and luxurious demand. She was sinking fast to a place where there was nothing but Reid and the glorious sensations only he could give her. She wanted to lose herself in them. Her heart had never raced this fast. Her body had never pulsed so desperately. Even in her wildest fantasies, she'd never conceived of feeling this way. And it still wasn't enough. She needed more. Everything. Him. Digging her fingers into his shoulders, she pulled him closer.

Big mistake. In some far corner of Reid's mind, the words blinked like a huge neon sign. They'd started sending their message the instant he'd told her that they would settle what was happening between them now. He'd gotten out of the car to gain some distance, some perspective. Some resolve. But the brief respite had only seemed to increase the seductive pull Nell had on him.

He'd been a goner the moment he'd stuffed himself back into the front seat.

Long before that.

Oh, her argument had been flawless. Knowing ex-

actly what you were up against was key in his job. Reid
heartily wished it was her logic that had made his hands
streak into her hair and not the feelings that she'd been
arousing in him all day.

For seven years.

The hunger she'd triggered while she'd been talking so logically felt as if it had been buried inside him
forever. Then once her lips had pressed against his, he
forgot everything except that he was finally kissing
her. Finally touching her hair. He hadn't imagined how
silky the texture would be. One hand remained there,
trapped, while the other roamed freely, moving down
and over her, memorizing the curves and angles in one
possessive stroke.

She was everything a man could wish for; as small,
slim, and supple as he'd imagined. And he'd imagined
a lot.

Her lips were soft, too. Inviting, accepting, arousing—just as he'd fantasized. The first taste had been
sweet. Just as he had expected. But when he changed
the angle and used his tongue to probe farther, to tease
and to tempt, her flavors grew darker, stronger, hotter.
And beneath all those layers, he tasted not surrender
but demand. He had no choice but to answer it, taking
them both deeper until all he knew was her. His desire
only grew until it was huge and consuming. Not to be
denied. He wanted her—no, he needed her the way
a man needed sleep after a day of labor; the way he
needed water after a drought.

Unable to stop himself, he took more. Her hands
were on his shoulders, gripping hard. He wanted them
on his bare skin so that he could feel the softness of her

palms, the scrape of her fingers. Even through the layers of clothing, she made him burn.

Reid knew he had to get a grip or that burn would sear right through him and leave a scar. No other woman had ever seduced him this way: body, mind, soul. He'd never allowed it. He shouldn't allow it now. But he couldn't stop himself from releasing her seat belt. His hands gripped her waist, lifted.

A series of staccato blasts from a horn had him dropping her back into her seat. Reid glanced around, spotted a sedan two slots down in the row facing them with its lights blinking, the horn blasting. Behind it, a woman fumbled with her keys and managed to quiet the alarm.

Emotions shot through him. Relief that the noise had been caused by a woman who'd accidentally set off her car alarm. Fear that it could have been worse. Anger at himself that he'd let Nell so thoroughly distract him again.

He brought his gaze back to her. "Now we know what it's like." And the knowledge could change everything if he let it.

Perhaps it already had.

Nell felt like a diver resurfacing layer by layer from a very great depth. Her head was reeling. Good thing he hadn't asked a question. Since her lips were once more not taking commands from her brain, she wouldn't have been able to answer.

In contrast he seemed to be doing fine—except for the grunt he made as he extricated himself from his side of the car. She waited where she was, praying that her brain cells would click on and that she'd be able to move by the time he circled to open her door.

When he did, he didn't offer his hand as he had at

the fast-food restaurant. Instead, he stepped back while she made it out on her own. She tested her legs, while she pressed the remote to lock the door.

"One more thing," he said.

She met his eyes.

"Now that we know what it's like, we're going to put it in a file and forget it." Then he turned, scanned the area and gestured her forward.

Wanna bet? Once more she was grateful that she didn't trust herself to speak. What *she* knew was that she now had two conflicting narratives to deal with. In one her goal was to find a long-missing necklace, and in the other, her goal was to seduce Reid Sutherland. Plot and subplot. All she had to do was find a way to weave them together.

7

NELL STOOD IN front of a long glass window. Beyond it Deanna Lewis lay in a narrow hospital bed flanked by serious-looking machines that beeped and blinked continuously. A nurse was in the room replacing an IV.

Ever since they'd left the car, Reid had slipped back into the role of Secret Service agent. He'd introduced himself and shown his badge to the young officer who was standing guard at Deanna Lewis's door. Officer Jameson had been polite, but he'd asked them to wait while he contacted his superior officer.

Signaling them to join him, the young man said, "Sheriff Skinner over in Glen Loch has cleared you."

Reid nodded to him, then turned as the nurse opened the door. "How is Miss Lewis?"

"There's been no change in her condition since the surgery." The woman's name tag read Nancy Braxton. Nell estimated she was in her late twenties. Leading them back into the room, Braxton continued, "Dr. Knight stops in to see her every day. He's confident that she's healing, but there's no way to tell when she might come out of the coma."

"And there have been no visitors?" Reid asked.

"No. The police have been quite explicit about that. The only people who have been allowed in this room are doctors, nurses or members of our volunteer staff."

"There was a reporter from the *New York Times* who stopped by last week," Officer Jameson said from the doorway. "I told him about the no-visitor policy."

"A reporter?" Reid asked.

"Very polite young man. James Orbison," Jameson said.

"Can you describe him?" Reid asked.

"Medium height, short brown hair, slender build," Jameson said.

"Cute," Nurse Braxton added. "He wore preppy clothes, and the glasses added a geeky aura. Sexy."

Jameson glanced at the nurse with a raised eyebrow. "Sexy?"

Braxton shrugged. "Just saying."

Reid interrupted the byplay. "Anything else you can recall?"

"He said he'd written an article about Castle MacPherson a little over six months ago," Jameson said. "He'd convinced his editor to let him do a follow-up piece once some of the Stuart sapphires were discovered."

"You didn't let him visit Ms. Lewis?"

"No. He did see her through the glass. No way to prevent that. And he had questions about her condition. But I told him that he'd have to talk to Sheriff Skinner over in Glen Loch if he wanted any further information. He said that the sheriff was next on his list." Jameson's gaze shifted to Deanna. "She's such a pretty little thing. It's hard to believe that she threatened to kill someone."

Nell agreed with the young officer's assessment. Even with her head wrapped in bandages, Deanna Lewis was pretty. Hooked up to all the tubes and wires, she looked fragile and defenseless. Yet she'd taken out Duncan with a Taser shot and then kidnapped Piper at gunpoint.

"You mentioned that members of the volunteer staff are allowed in the room," Reid said. "Who are they exactly?"

"Oh, we have an amazing group of people who volunteer their services here at the hospital," Nurse Braxton said. "Many of them are senior citizens, but we also have college students who are required to do community service as part of their degree programs. Since Deanna didn't have any family visiting, Dr. Knight asked the woman who runs the service if she could find someone to spend time reading to her. He believes that the sound of a human voice often speeds the recovery of coma patients."

"And the volunteers do that?" Reid asked.

"One volunteer," Nurse Braxton said. "After her first visit, she said she'd try to come back every day. But the day before yesterday, she said she had to go out of town for a couple of days and not to expect her back for a few days."

Nell glanced at Reid, and she could tell what he was thinking. She asked the question. "What did this woman look like?"

"Brunette, tall and very attractive. In her early fifties, I'd say. Well dressed. Good jewelry."

"Did you notice a ring on her finger?" Nell asked.

Nurse Braxton nodded. "Yes. A gold one with a kind

of crest on it. I remarked on it. She said it was the family coat of arms."

"*Gwen* was on her name tag," Officer Jameson said. "She signed in as G. Harris."

Reid turned to him. "Was she ever alone with the patient?"

"No, sir. I always left the door open when she came, just as I'm doing now. All Ms. Harris did was read to her. The same book each time. A children's story with pictures. Sometimes she'd read it more than once."

"Do you remember what the story was about?" Nell asked. But she was pretty sure she already knew.

"It was a fairy tale about this Scot who stole his true love away from her family, brought her to the New World and built her a castle with a magical stone arch. Made me think of the one over at Castle MacPherson."

NELL WAS ASLEEP beside him when Reid turned down the dirt road that wound its way to the castle. He'd updated Duncan and Sheriff Skinner in Glen Loch before they'd left the hospital and then insisted on driving Nell's car.

If Gwen Harris showed up again at the hospital, Officer Jameson or whoever was on guard would contact Skinner discretely. Reid and Nell hadn't discussed what they'd learned; in fact, they'd barely spoken since they'd left the traffic of Albany behind. He could tell that, before she'd drifted off, she'd been doing exactly what he was doing—running through the possible explanations for the information they had gathered from their visit to the hospital. Nell's subconscious mind was probably still busily looking at the various story lines while she slept. The problem was there were too many possibilities, and so far they couldn't prove even one.

As the car crested a steep hill, he shifted his attention to the view. Below lay a postcard snapshot of Castle MacPherson tucked into the mountains on a rocky promontory overlooking a quiet blue lake. The image perfectly matched the one he'd carried around in his mind for seven years. The three stories of gray stone stood sturdy and strong, the sun glinting off its windows. Gardens stretched to the west, high cliffs to the east. He even caught a glimpse of Angus's legendary stone arch at the edge of the gardens before the road took the final steep dip that ended at the castle drive.

As he pressed down on the brake for a sharp curve, he glanced over at Nell. She slept like a child, her hand tucked beneath her cheek on the car door. Keeping her safe had to be his top priority, but he wasn't at all sure he could keep her safe from him.

File it away and forget it.

Excellent plan. Too bad he didn't have a chance in hell of sticking to it. When they'd tried that experimental kiss, *desire* seemed too tame a word for the gut-deep, soul-searing arousal he'd experienced. That wasn't the part that scared him the most. What did was that, at some point while he'd been kissing her, he'd wanted to give her more. He'd wanted to deny her nothing.

If that woman in the hospital parking lot hadn't accidentally set off the alarm in her car, he would have made love to Nell right in the front seat of her Fiat. He'd never done anything quite that reckless in his entire life. Not even when his teenage hormones had been at their peak.

Just the thought of it tempted him to pull off onto a side road, find a spot that was a bit more private and finish what he'd started in the parking lot. Reckless and impulsive were qualities he ruthlessly suppressed. Now Nell was making him want to set them free.

Even more troubling was what he had felt when she had mentioned the man she'd fallen in love with. Jealousy. The coppery taste in his mouth, the wrench in his gut—both had been unprecedented.

He might be able to get out of this unscathed. If he dropped her at the castle and never saw her again. That scenario wasn't open to him.

But if they started down the path where their desires were leading them, he didn't see a happy ending for either of them.

He didn't want to hurt her. She was young and idealistic, and she had this incredibly sunny outlook on life. There was no way she wouldn't expect a happy-ever-after. And she should have it. In many ways, she'd always reminded him a bit of his mother. He'd seen, perhaps more than his brothers ever had, the kind of pain she'd suffered when she'd learned that their father had never loved her. Reid never wanted to be responsible for hurting anyone the way his father had hurt all of them. Better not to go there. Nell deserved someone who would love her and have a family with her.

Ahead of him, the road leveled and the crunch of gravel beneath the tires told him that he was on the driveway. The moment he turned the car around the curve, he spotted Viola MacPherson just outside the front door. The dog sitting at her feet had to be Alba. Cam had filled him in on the dog that Vi had brought home from a shelter when she'd starting hearing noises in the middle of the night.

The fact that Alba was deaf made her a strange choice as a watchdog, but her instincts had turned out to be spot-on, because she had exposed the con man threatening Adair's life and wanting Eleanor's sapphire earring.

Reid shifted his gaze to the tall man with the silver-streaked hair standing next to Vi—Cam's boss at the CIA, Daryl Garnett. Reid knew Cam thought the world of him.

He pulled the car to a stop, then put his hand on Nell's. "Nell?"

Even before she turned her head, her fingers linked with his. Her eyes opened, and as he looked into them, Reid felt himself being pulled into that world where only the two of them existed. He'd felt desire before. And he'd experienced passion. But nothing this intense. Nothing this irresistible.

Then Vi was opening the passenger door and in seconds, the two women were in each other's arms, both talking over the other. The dog circled them once and then sat to watch.

When Reid climbed out of the car, Vi broke away from Nell long enough to envelope him in a hug. "Welcome back to Castle MacPherson." Then she turned to draw her niece into the house.

"They're going to need a few minutes," Daryl said. "Vi says she hasn't seen Nell for nearly a year because of that grant. In the meantime, I've got good news and bad news. Can I offer you a beer to wash both down?"

Reid smiled at him and extended his hand. "Cam said I was going to like you."

IT TOOK HALF a bottle of beer, but Reid was feeling more relaxed than he had all day. He and Daryl were seated at a table on the terrace outside the kitchen. Over

Daryl's shoulder, Reid could see the sun streaking the sky with pink as it sank closer to the lake. He'd been formally introduced to Alba, who'd sniffed his hand and then stretched out in a waning patch of sunlight and fallen asleep. Beyond her, through the glass of the terrace doors, he could see Vi and Nell chatting as they put together a meal.

"Vi roasted a chicken," Daryl said. "I think that's her version of killing the fatted calf."

Reid raised a brow. "If that's the good news, I'd rather it was related to the case."

Daryl grinned at him. "Vi's cooking is always good news. And she's celebrating the fact that the last of the Sutherland boys has finally returned to the castle. She's always thought of you three in a very special way, and since you're the final triplet to come back, that gives you prodigal son status. Don't knock it. As I recall, Cam got sandwiches, and Duncan had to grill his own steak."

Reid laughed. "Do me a favor and pass the word along to Cam about the chicken. It will just reinforce my status as the favored eldest son. But now, tell me you have something on Gwendolen Campbell."

"I do. Duncan forwarded me the text you sent him from the hospital, and once I had the name, it didn't take long to ID her. She had her name changed legally to Campbell six months ago. Before that, she was Gwendolen Harris."

"The name she used at the hospital when she was visiting Deanna Lewis."

"Turns out it isn't the only name she's gone by. Gerald Harris, the fifth Earl of Bainbridge, was her third husband," Daryl said. "He was twenty years her senior, and she inherited millions when he died."

"Explains the expensive clothes and jewelry."

"Husband number two, Martin Hatcher, wasn't short on money, either. Marrying him got her United States citizenship and she got his money when he passed on."

"Sounds like a pattern," Reid said.

"The pattern of a good grifter. But there's more. Husband number one was Douglas Lewis, and Deanna was just three years old when her widowed father married Gwen. Gwendolen's maiden name was MacDonald, and she was Douglas Lewis's second wife. That's why we didn't run across Gwendolen before this. Cam has discovered that she was born and raised in a village not twenty miles away from what remains of the Campbell estate in Scotland. He and Adair are looking into that end of it. But MacDonald isn't one of the names that pops up on the Campbell family tree that your mother discovered."

Reid took a swallow of his beer. "So this Gwendolen MacDonald Lewis Hatcher Harris is Deanna Lewis's stepmother. That would explain the visits to the hospital and offers a reason why they might be working together. But the question remains. Who is the man, or woman, who tried to run Piper down earlier today and how does he—or she—fit into the family picture?"

"We don't know yet. That's the bad news. Duncan says his friend at the police department will send us a rendering of the police artist's sketch of the hit-and-run driver as soon as it's completed. Then I'll give it to Sheriff Skinner, and he'll show it to Edie at the diner."

Reid grinned. "Edie is still running the diner?"

"She is, and besides serving up the best pancakes in upstate New York, she also provides better local information than the internet. If anyone who looks like this guy shows up, we'll get the news. It's her granddaughter Molly who's getting married here on Saturday, so Edie is especially interested in seeing that everything runs smoothly."

Reid sipped his beer. "Can we provide enough security for the wedding?"

"It's very small, and everyone is local. It will be impossible for someone to slip in unnoticed. The only outsider who might be attending is a young reporter from the *New York Times*, the one who did the original article that helped launch Castle MacPherson as a prime wedding destination."

"If you're talking about James Orbison, he dropped by the hospital to check on Deanna Lewis," Reid said.

"Sheriff Skinner told me. Last week Orbison dropped by to see him, and he also contacted Vi to arrange an interview tomorrow. He wants to shadow her for the day. I've done a background check, and he seems squeaky clean. He has a degree in journalism from Princeton. His uncle is a senior editor for the Sunday *Times* magazine section, and James started working for him right after graduation. We can meet him when he comes to interview Vi tomorrow."

"I want to ask him why he decided to write the original article on the castle."

Setting down his beer, Daryl said, "One more thing. Now that we know there's a connection between Deanna and Gwendolen and something about who they are, I've put some old friends of mine on it—a couple retired agents who are over in England. They're going to work with Cam and Adair."

Reid met Daryl's eyes. "They're going to have to

be fast. I'm not sure we have as much time as they've given us."

"What do you mean?"

Reid glanced to his right where he could see Nell and Vi moving about the kitchen. "Nell has this idea that she and her sisters are somehow destined to find the Stuart sapphires."

Daryl thought for a moment. "You think she's right?"

"I favor more practical scenarios, but I can't dismiss her idea," Reid said. "It sure didn't take Adair and Piper long to discover the two earrings once they returned to the castle. It was almost as if they'd been drawn to them like magnets. If Nell's right, she could discover the necklace very soon. Then she'll be disposable. If she doesn't find it fast, Vi could be in danger. That means that we can't let either of these women out of our sight, until we've got all the players behind bars."

He gestured to the two women in the kitchen. "As Nell has pointed out to me several times today—the clock is ticking."

"I hear you," Daryl said. "If there's one thing I've learned in the past few weeks, it's that things tend to move quickly here. I have one piece of advice to give you."

Reid turned to meet the older man's gaze.

Daryl smiled. "Beware of the legend. If you don't intend to marry a MacPherson woman, don't let her kiss you beneath the stones."

8

I'M HOME, NELL thought as she trimmed the ends off string beans and added them to a pot of water. A few feet away, Aunt Vi took a roasting pan out of the oven and placed it on top of the stove to cool. The scent of the chicken and freshly baked scones surrounded her with comfort and a feeling of safety. She'd spent her childhood, her girlhood, her adolescence, in this room. On rainy days, she'd played Scrabble with her sisters at the counter. Under her aunt's supervision, she had finished math assignments and had written her first short story at the kitchen table. After rinsing her hands in the sink, Nell sank into a chair to watch her aunt mash a steaming pot of potatoes. "You're making a feast."

Vi glanced up. "Tomorrow will be busy. There's a rehearsal for the wedding on Saturday. Very small. Edie's granddaughter Molly is getting married. So we're having a family celebration tonight. Reid hasn't visited since your father's wedding, and it's been nearly a year since you've been here—your longest absence yet. Your sisters were surprised that you completed your grant work. Very proud and pleased—but surprised."

Nell grinned at her. "Did they expect me to get homesick and run back here?"

"Something like that. They were worried when you turned down that part-time teaching position at Huntleigh College. They saw it as the perfect job to complement your writing career."

"And it would have kept me wrapped in a cocoon. I loved every minute of the year I spent on my own—no dorm supervisor, no one to report to except myself. No one to depend on except myself."

"No one hovering over you. The butterfly breaks free." Vi nodded in understanding. "You always had at least three of us looking out for you, telling you what to do."

Nell laughed. "*You* never hovered. You were much more subtle than Piper and Adair."

"I learned early on that it didn't do much good to argue with you once you had your mind made up. You were always your own boss, Nell. When you know what you want, you go after it, and you usually get it. So besides celebrating your independence, what did you enjoy the most on your cross-country tour?"

Nell smiled. "The settings, the people, and I kept a daily log. Now I have so much that will enrich my writing. I'm trying my hand at writing a different kind of book this time. Romantic suspense for adults. It will be very different from my first."

Vi glanced over her shoulder. "I'm not surprised that you're taking on a new challenge. But it seems to me that *It's All Good* shares many qualities of the genre. Eleanor is a strong woman—just the kind of heroine a reader would connect with in a romantic suspense novel. As for Angus—he's a classic hero. He swept his true love off her feet and carried her off."

Nell thought of how different their situation was from her own. Fat chance that Reid was going to sweep her off her feet. In fact, she suspected that she was the one who was going to have to do the sweeping. "That makes Eleanor sound like a wimp. I want my heroine to be stronger."

"Don't sell Eleanor short. She left everything to go with Angus—her family, her home, the life she knew. To my way of thinking, that took a lot of courage."

Vi glanced through the glass terrace doors at the two men and then turned back to Nell. "They're about halfway through their beers. How about we have a glass of wine, and you can tell me what you're going to do about Reid Sutherland, and how you're going to find the necklace."

Nell tilted her head, studying her aunt as she opened a chilled bottle of white wine and filled two glasses. She hadn't missed the fact that Reid had come first on her aunt's list and not the necklace. "Reid's always been your favorite of the Sutherland boys, hasn't he?"

"He accepted the responsibility of taking care of my girls. You played a lot of risky games that summer."

Nell grinned. "You weren't supposed to know about them."

After taking a sip of her wine, Vi poured warm milk into the pot with the potatoes, then continued to mash. "It was my job to know. And I worried less because of Reid. He and his brothers were ten. And they were boys through and through. Mischief was in their genes. Reid could have made it his entire focus that summer to have fun. Instead, he made it his responsibility to keep all of you safe."

"He became my hero. My Prince Charming. I fell in love with him that summer."

"I fell in love with him a bit, too," Vi admitted. "He won my heart the day that Cam and Duncan decided you were all going to hike up Stone Mountain and find the source of the water that drops over Tinker's Falls."

Nell frowned for a bit as she searched her memory. "I remember we played at the falls a lot and in the cave where Piper and Duncan discovered the second earring, but I don't recall going to Stone Mountain."

"That's because you and Reid didn't go. He let his brothers go off with Adair and Piper. They were eight and nine. You were six. So he talked you into a day of playing tea party with your animals and dolls. I can't imagine that was the way he preferred to spend his time."

Nell grinned. "Now I remember that day. No one had been willing to play tea party with me before. Adair and Piper were always fascinated by the more dangerous games the boys came up with."

"Reid knew exactly what bait to use to keep you from feeling you were missing out on the big adventure. I figured then he had to be pretty good at keeping watch over his brothers."

Nell shifted her gaze to the two men on the terrace. Vi's description of Reid rang true. He was a natural-born caretaker and it made him very good at his job. "He's still very much a protector."

"I'm depending on that." Vi set the pot of potatoes on a burner and sat down next to her niece.

A line appeared on Nell's brow as she continued to

study Reid speculatively. "That's posing a bit of a challenge for me."

"A challenge?"

"A big one. I was drawn to him when he was a boy because he was handsome and kind, a storybook hero. A fantasy in the flesh. Now what he makes me feel is entirely different. He stirs things up in me I didn't know were there. I didn't even know they were possible. I've never felt about anyone the way I feel about him."

Vi took Nell's hands in hers. "Does he know how you feel?"

"Oh, yes. And the stirring-up part is mutual. That's when our narratives start to conflict."

"How?"

"He's not happy about it. He doesn't want to hurt me. He thinks we should file away what we're feeling and what we could feel, and forget all about it. If Angus had been that kind of hero, this castle wouldn't be here. And neither would all of us."

Vi smiled at her. "You obviously take issue with Reid's solution."

Nell shifted her gaze to Reid again. "I do. I only have to look at him to want him. And I can't stop thinking about how much more we could stir up in each other. He kissed me today for the first time. I'm hoping that the forbidden-fruit thing kicks in, and he won't be able to resist taking another bite. I definitely want to kiss him again, and I want to know what comes next."

"Have you decided what you're going to do about it?" Vi asked.

"Yes." Nell thought of the scenarios she'd plotted out and hidden away on the night of their parents' wedding, and of all the other similar ones that had fueled her dreams for years.

Vi patted her hand. "Good. I'd act fast. That's what I did with Daryl."

Nell's eyes widened. "You did?"

"I did." She grinned at her niece. "I knew I wanted him the first time I looked at him, so I took him out to the stone arch and kissed him there on the first day we met."

Nell laughed as she hugged her aunt. "Well, that's not my plan with Reid. He's made it clear that he doesn't want the happy-ever-after part."

"What do you want?"

"More than anything I want to enjoy what he and I can have together right now. And I have a plan."

"Of course you do. But don't kiss him beneath the stones. Not until you're sure you want the happy-ever-after part." Vi took another sip of her wine. "Do you know what you're going to do about Eleanor's necklace?"

"Working on it." She slipped her hand into her pocket and pulled out a folded piece of pink paper. "Remember Mom's old jewelry box that Adair and Piper and I used to bury our goals and dreams in?"

"The one you buried in the stone arch? The one I wasn't supposed to know anything about?"

Nell laughed. "You knew everything we did, and you let us do it."

"So you've written down your goal to find Eleanor's necklace, and you're going to tap into the power of the stone arch to help you. That's a brilliant plan."

Nell glanced through the glass doors at Reid. Using the stone arch to facilitate finding Eleanor's necklace was only half of her plan. She had another piece of pink paper in her pocket. On that one she'd written her goal to seduce Reid and turn into reality the fantasies she'd written seven years ago. That way she could weave plot and subplot together. Since she could hardly seduce a man who wasn't around, any plan she might have entertained of slipping away from Reid and trying to find the necklace on her own would have to be modified. She'd have to work with him. She intended to place both papers in the jewelry box tonight because the clock was ticking.

THE CLOCK ON the parlor mantel struck the first of eleven bongs when Vi smothered a yawn and said, "Well, I'm ready to call it a night." Alba rose from her relaxed position in front of the fireplace and moved to Vi's side.

"When you hit a brick wall, sometimes the best cure is a good night's sleep," Daryl said.

They'd hit a brick wall all right, Nell thought as she hugged her aunt, and then Daryl surprised her by kissing her on the cheek. After dinner, they'd retired to the main parlor, reviewing everything they knew, didn't know, guessed or speculated.

Vi had even set up one of the whiteboards from Adair's office so that they could map out everything that had happened along a time line. However, at the end of more than two hours of studying the chronology of events, discussing, and theorizing, they weren't any further ahead than when they'd started. Reid followed Daryl out of the room. From the corner of her eye, Nell saw the two men pause to talk at the foot of the main staircase. Protection strategies, she thought.

There wasn't a doubt in her mind that Reid expected

her to join them so that he could escort her up to her room and "file her away" for the night.

Not happening. To distract herself from the flutter of nerves in her stomach, she moved closer to Eleanor's portrait. There was a part of her that envied the woman for having a lover who simply swept her away. The old Nell would have been thrilled by that. Recalling her aunt's comments on Eleanor's strength, she studied the painting more closely. At first glance, Eleanor appeared the same: beautiful, serene and very happy. But there was no denying the look of determination in her eyes, the lift to her chin.

All Nell needed was half the guts it had taken Eleanor to leave her family and home in Scotland to run away with her true love. Not that she intended to run away with Reid. All she wanted to do was give in to the yearning that had been growing inside her since the first time she'd seen him.

If Eleanor had felt this way about Angus, no wonder she'd risked everything to be with him. Again Nell checked the doorway to the main parlor. No sign of Reid. She glanced back up at the portrait and whispered, "At least you didn't have to deal with a reluctant lover."

REID WAITED UNTIL Daryl had disappeared around the curve of the landing before he turned and walked toward the open door of the main parlor. He'd successfully avoided being alone with Nell since they'd arrived at the castle. Not that the strategy had helped him control his preoccupation with her. While they'd been discussing the case for that last hour, he'd entirely lost the thread of the conversation. Twice.

That wasn't like him at all. In his job, he couldn't afford to lose his focus. Even when she wasn't looking at him, he still felt her in every pore of his being, and he felt that same sense of connection, which bordered on recognition, that he'd felt when they'd stood together beneath the stone arch seven years ago.

The Nell he'd known when he was ten was simple. The Nell he was coming to know was complex. He liked the way she looked—the delicate features, the fair skin, the hair that reminded him of spun gold. He also was coming to like and admire the way her mind worked. The problem was, the longer he was with her, the more he learned about her, the more fascinating she became.

He half hoped that she'd follow them out into the hallway, so that he could escort her safely up to her room and retire to his own. Separation and some distance were what he needed.

Right.

He wasn't a man who lied to himself. *Half hoped* were two telling words. There was a part of him that had wanted her to linger in the parlor so that he could be alone with her. Even though it meant playing with fire. Reid shoved his hands into his pockets. That wasn't like him, either. At least it hadn't been like him in a long time. Not since he and his brothers had been eight and they'd literally played with some matches they'd found in a kitchen drawer. Their father had been away, their mother working in her office. And she'd left him in charge. Her words had been, "Don't let your brothers burn down the house—or worse."

Cam had initiated the disaster by striking the first match. Then Duncan, usually the one to remain on the sidelines, had joined in. Finally Reid had succumbed to the hypnotic power of the bright flames. Their little adventure had progressed quickly from striking individual matches to starting a small blaze in a wastebasket which had severely damaged one wall of kitchen cabinets before the fire department arrived on the scene to put it out.

Even more than the scorched wood, he regretted the look of disappointment in his mother's eyes.

But he wasn't eight years old anymore. Dammit. Nell was changing him. There was something in her that tempted him to give in to that streak of recklessness that he suspected he and his brothers had inherited from his father. He wasn't sure he could resist her any more than he'd been able to resist striking that match on that long-ago afternoon. What he was absolutely certain of was that, if he started this particular fire, disaster lay ahead.

He didn't move into the room when he spoke. "You're not ready to call it a night yet."

"No." She flicked him a glance, then turned her attention back to the painting. "I want to start looking for the necklace."

"Tonight?"

"The clock is ticking. And this portrait is part of the story. For years it's been the only evidence that the sapphires exist. I think there's something in it that might provide a clue."

Intrigued, Reid joined her in front of the painting. "Why do you think that?"

"It's always been called her wedding portrait, but that can't be what it really is. True, she's wearing a white dress and there are flowers in her hair. But she and Angus ran away." Nell gestured to the upper right-hand corner of the painting. "You can see the stone arch that Angus built for her. So she sat for this portrait after they'd been here awhile. In my book, they married onboard the ship that brought them here. I had them renew their wedding vows beneath the arch once it was completed."

"In celebration of their first anniversary," Reid murmured.

She turned to stare at him. "You read *It's All Good?*"

He picked up a strand of her hair and rubbed it between his fingers. "Several times. I enjoyed it. Their story has always intrigued me, and you captured the heart of it in your book."

When she said nothing and continued to stare at him, he said, "You seem surprised that I enjoyed it."

"I'm trying to imagine you reading a children's story."

He smiled then. Because he wanted badly to do more than touch her hair, he dropped the strand and turned to the portrait. "Eleanor has always fascinated me. That summer when you and your sisters first showed us this painting and told us her story, my brothers immediately focused on finding the missing jewels. I was struck by the woman."

He had to wonder if that was because, even then, she made him think of the woman Nell would become. They had the same gold hair, pale skin, delicate features, stubborn chin. And the mouth. Eleanor's lips were slightly parted as if they were just waiting for a lover's kiss. His mind slipped back to that moment in the car when he'd been staring at Nell's mouth and nothing had mattered to him but kissing her. And more.

He could so easily have more. She was standing close enough that, if either of them moved, he would feel the brush of her body against his. If he turned ever so slightly, he could pull her into his arms. She wouldn't resist, and he could once more lose himself in the explosive heat of her response. Lose himself in her.

He shifted his gaze to the necklace. That was what he should be thinking about. "Perhaps the painting does hold the key. If we assume she was the one who hid them—"

"She did," Nell interrupted. "I'm certain of it."

"Why? Why not just pass them on to her heirs?"

Nell frowned at the portrait. "According to the story that was passed down, the jewels were Eleanor's dowry. But Deanna Lewis told Piper that they didn't belong to Eleanor, that she and whoever her partner was had a stronger claim. Maybe Eleanor felt the same way—that the jewels really did belong to someone else. After all, she eloped with Angus. That suggests that he may not have been someone her family approved of."

"Interesting."

"Deanna and Gwendolen may hold the answer."

He glanced at her. "What about your theory that you and your sisters are meant to find them? How does that fit?"

"I don't know exactly. But if I were going to hide something as beautiful as those jewels, I'd leave a clue. What better place to put it than in this portrait? Maybe that's why she had it painted in the first place and why she wore the sapphires. It's probably why this painting has survived all these years."

"Good point." Reid used her theory to study the portrait through a new lens. This time instead of focusing on Eleanor and her jewels, he concentrated on the other details. "She's sitting in the garden on a bench. There's a pile of books or notebooks next to her."

"Sketch pads, I'm betting. She drew," Nell said. "All of the illustrations in my book are based on her sketches."

"I read about that. The two of you share a talent for bringing images vividly to life. The location of that spot is somewhere in the gardens within sight of the stone arch, but I don't recall that latticework directly behind her."

"My father believed she was sitting in the gazebo," Nell said. "The wood structure rotted away years ago, but the stone foundation is still there." She sent him a smile. "You should remember it. You spent a day there playing tea party with me."

"What I remember is a pile of rocks."

"Beauty is in the eye of the beholder." Nell took a step back. "And so is the clue to the location of the necklace if we could just see it."

Still intrigued, he continued to study the painting. To hell with talking her into going to bed and getting a fresh start in the morning. His best strategy was to indulge her desire to be independent and encourage her to take the lead. And maybe it was time he surprised her. "If your theory is right and Eleanor is pointing the way to the jewels in this portrait, you'll want to start at the stone arch. Let's go out there right now."

She turned to stare at him. "I was going to suggest that, but I was sure you'd argue."

He grinned at her. "Waste of time. You were going to make the point that, as long as the autograph lady and company are depending on you to lead them to the necklace, you'll be safe. And if someone *is* out there watching, they'll see you're doing exactly what they want."

She shot him a frown as they moved out of the room. "I don't like that you can practically read my mind."

The feeling was mutual, but he wasn't about to admit that to her. Instead, he said, "Your mind works in a very logical way."

Her smile held a hint of mischief. "Not always. I think it's time that I filled you in on the fantasy box that my sisters and I buried in the stones a long time ago."

9

"I'VE ALWAYS LOVED the gardens," Nell said. "Especially at this time of night. All I have to do is take a breath and I can almost taste the roses and the freesias."

All Reid could smell was Nell, and his desire to taste her again was growing with each step they took. In spite of his belief that their trip to the stone arch put her in minimal danger, he still kept himself alert.

The full moon gleamed off the lake, and stars, undimmed by city lights, sparkled in the clear sky overhead. The illumination provided by Mother Nature made them fairly visible to anyone who might have stationed themselves in the hills that jutted up on three sides of the grounds. There could be someone up there right now, keeping an eye on the castle and specifically on Nell's movements.

When a sudden turn in the path caused her to brush against his arm, the desire that simmered constantly now in his blood shot to full boil. His awareness, previously attuned to their surroundings, narrowed to her as swiftly and dramatically as a spotlight on a stage. God, he wanted to touch her, really touch her. To slip that drab little suit off her and let his hands slowly, very slowly, mold every inch of her. Temptation grew as he imagined just how quickly he could edge her off the path and into the cover provided by the flowering trees that filled this particular part of the gardens. He wanted to give in to it—to throw caution to the wind, pull her into the shadows and just take her. It would be wonderfully crazy, and the certainty that she wouldn't resist him—that she'd deny him nothing—gave an unprecedented power to the images filling his mind. He might have made them a reality, if they hadn't stepped into the clearing in front of the stone arch.

Reid had to blink against brightness of the floodlights trained on the stones. They'd been installed after someone had planted a bomb inside the arch, once the first earring had been discovered. That person had nearly killed Alba. The sudden memory dragged him back to the real danger that still threatened Nell and her family.

When she started forward, he took her arm. "Let's keep to the edge of the light until we have to step into it."

"This is the first time I've seen them lit up like that. I think Angus would have liked it."

Reid recalled the first time he'd seen the stone arch. At ten he'd been impressed with the structure. It was a tunnel, really—ten feet long, ten high in the center and eight feet wide. He and his brothers had measured it off. It impressed him no less now that it was lit up like a monument. He was even more impressed with the man who'd built it. It had lasted two hundred years, and it would be here for years to come. So would the legend. "Not many men leave behind such a legacy."

"It's a real tribute to the power of love," Nell said.

"That kind of love is rare," Reid said. "A lot of people want it, but very few achieve it." He should tell her again that it wasn't in the cards for them. She had to want the rarified kind of love.

His mother certainly had. And now it seemed she'd found it with A.D., and Nell's aunt and sisters had found chances at their own happy-ever-afters. A.D. was a good man. So was Daryl. Cam and Duncan were good men. They'd never promise what they didn't think they could deliver on. But if the stats held true, two out of the four of those couples would be denied what they most desired. That's what he needed to tell her.

Before he could, she said, "I couldn't agree more. Even the few who are lucky enough to find true love can have it snatched away and be nearly destroyed by the loss. My father's a prime example of that. When my mother died, my sisters and I lost him, too. He was so devastated that he hid away in his rooms painting. I was too young to understand at the time, but when I finally did, I decided that true love isn't worth the risk. Not to mention the drama and the stress. And even with the legend, there are no guarantees."

Hadn't he always felt the same way? Why did it bother him that she'd simply voiced his own assessment? Or perhaps he was just annoyed by the impossibility of arguing with someone who shared his opinion.

Nell took a deep breath and told herself to shut up. She'd made her point, and she was starting to babble. The walk through the garden had taken its toll on her concentration. She'd lied about loving the scent of the roses and the freesias. She'd barely noticed them compared to Reid. He smelled of soap: simple, basic. Wonderful. When he'd accidentally brushed up against her arm, she'd lost her train of thought completely.

Not good.

She needed to keep her head as clear as one of her heroines if she was going to achieve all her goals tonight. Slipping her hand into her pocket, she fingered the two slips of pink paper that had been burning a hole there all evening. The action helped her refocus.

They reached the far end of the clearing where the distance to the opening of the stone arch was only about twenty-five yards away. She needed to get to the fantasy box. "My sisters and I used to sneak out here late at night when we thought Aunt Vi was asleep. The instant we stepped out of the gardens, we always used to race for the stones." She flicked him a look. "Bet I can beat you." She took off.

The element of surprise should have guaranteed her a victory. But Reid was fast, his reflexes honed to perfection. He clamped a hand on her arm within the first ten yards, and they ended the race in a tie. When they finally stood beneath the arch, she was breathing hard. He wasn't.

"You've got to remember to let me do my bodyguarding thing." His hand was still wrapped around her arm, but his grip was no longer as firm. So there was no reason at all for her to feel the pressure of each one of his fingers. Even less reason for her knees to turn to water.

Then she made the mistake of looking at him. He'd turned to scan the clearing, and the memory of him on their parent's wedding day superimposed itself over what she was seeing now. He'd been standing in profile that day, too. His hair had been longer then and more tousled. She'd wanted so much to touch it. To touch him. The urge had been so acute that if the bridal couple hadn't separated her from him, she was sure she would have.

Nothing separated them right now. They were alone. She could do exactly what she'd wanted to do that afternoon seven years ago, what she'd started to do in the hospital parking lot. All she had to do was lift her hand. But when she pulled it out of her pocket, she was holding the two slips of pink paper, and her grip on reality and her goals came back into focus. First things first.

"Nell…"

She met his eyes, and for a moment she wavered. It would be so easy to step into his arms and kiss him again. So easy to just lose herself in that whirlwind of excitement that was waiting for her. She certainly wanted to. But if she did, they'd do more than kiss. Then he'd have second thoughts again, just as he had in the car. Worse still, he'd regret it. That was the kind of man she was dealing with. A man who lived by a very strict code. A man who didn't want to hurt her. A protector.

She was pretty sure that the fantasy she'd begun all those years ago was the perfect solution. But first she had to set up the story line.

"I have to tell you about these pink slips and the fantasy box," she said. "From the time we were little, my sisters and I used to sneak out here, write down our goals and dreams and put them into this metal box." Turning, she dropped to her knees and ran her hand along the base of the arch. "I'll show you."

Reid stayed right where he was, hoping to get a grip on his resolve. And his sanity. A moment ago, he'd nearly lost both. Dragging his eyes away from Nell, he glanced around the stone arch.

It would be dangerous and reckless to drag her into the shadows in the garden and make love to her. But to do the same thing beneath the arch that Angus MacPherson had built for his true love? That was just crazy.

Saved by two pieces of folded pink paper. And a box of fantasies?

Curious, he squatted down and tried to get a better look at what she was doing. "Can I help?"

Her first response was a grunt, followed by, "I think I've got it."

Stone scraped against stone. Then Nell turned, sat on her heels and set a small metal box on the stone floor. When she opened it, Reid saw that it was divided in three sections with folded sheets of colored paper in each one.

"It was Adair who thought of it." Nell explained her sister's plan. "To make it even more adventurous, we would all meet in Piper's room and then climb down from her balcony. Hers was closest to the ground."

As he listened, Reid was just as fascinated by the story as he was by the play of shadows and muted light on her face. She had a gift with words that drew vivid pictures of the three sisters climbing down the balcony, then racing through the gardens to bury their deepest and most heartfelt desires in the stones. He'd been touched when she'd told him that the box had originally been their mother's jewelry box. Amused when he'd learned that they'd each used a different color of paper to guard their privacy and that her color had turned out to be pink.

"Some of my goals were pretty frivolous," she admitted with a wry smile. "One of my early ones was to just be taller than my sisters."

"When did you achieve it?" Reid asked.

"Six years later. Of course, I was hoping for an overnight change. At twelve, I was wishing I'd set my sights higher. My sisters didn't offer much of a challenge in the height department."

Reid laughed. "With siblings it's always about competition and pecking order."

"Even with triplets?"

"Especially with triplets."

After glancing at the slips in her palm, she handed one of them to Reid. "I'm going to use the box again and tap into the power of the stones."

And it was going to work. Whatever doubts she'd had, whatever nerves plagued her had begun to fade the moment her fingers first brushed against her mother's jewelry box. There was a power here that had never failed her.

While he leaned toward the mouth of the arch to maximize the light, she glanced down at the folded pieces of pink paper she'd written her sexual fantasy on. They were easy to identify because all the other goals were written on small single sheets. She'd filled two large pieces of paper with her plans for Reid, and over the years she'd expanded them a lot.

"'My goal is to find Eleanor's sapphire necklace before sundown tomorrow,'" Reid read aloud. Then he refolded the slip of paper and passed it to her. "You're being more specific with your time frame, I see."

"A lesson learned the hard way." She placed the goal on the top of the pile.

"You really believe that putting that into the box

and tucking it into the stones is going to help you find the necklace?"

"I know it is. There's a power here." Positive of that, she placed the second slip of paper she'd brought on the top of her pile and closed the lid.

"Don't I get to read that one?"

"I'll tell you all about it." *Just as soon as I get it buried.* She slid the box into its niche and replaced the stones. Then, still on her knees, she faced him. "That final piece of paper was a sexual fantasy I wrote about you on the night our parents married."

"Nell—"

She stopped him by placing a hand over his lips. "Let me finish. I knew even then that you would be a reluctant lover, so I wrote about seducing you. I'd never before imagined myself in that kind of role, but with you it was easy. Let me turn that fantasy into reality. Just one night—no harm, no foul."

When he said nothing, she moved her hand to his shoulder, then down his arm and closed them around his fingers. Triumph thrilled her when his fingers gripped hers hard. "I've waited so long to touch you, and it's the perfect time. Once we find the necklace and everyone's safe, we'll go our separate ways. End of story."

"Life doesn't work like a story line, Nell. Shit happens."

"I'm a big girl. I can handle shit." She raised his hand to her mouth, kissed their linked fingers. Then she placed her free hand on his chest. His heart was beating as hard as hers. "My story line in my fantasy is all about enjoying each other for as long as we can."

With his free hand, he simply took a strand of her hair. "People leave."

"Of course they do." There was no mistaking the flash of pain she'd seen in his eyes. Odd that she'd never thought of Reid as being vulnerable. But it occurred to her that he might be just as afraid of being hurt as he was of hurting her.

Her instinct was to soothe. "People walk in and out of our lives all the time. I lost my mother before I could even remember her. Adair and Piper missed her terribly. But they at least had the memory of her. I don't. You and I can have each other now. I'd rather live with the memory of that than with regret, wouldn't you?"

Regrets. Reid was sure he'd have them. He already knew he wanted to give her more than she was asking for. More than he was capable of giving her. "You win."

When he leaned toward her, she placed a firm hand on his chest. "We have to find a better place for me to seduce you. We don't want the legend kicking in." Rising, she tugged him with her and stepped out of the stone arch. "In my fantasy, I started my seduction very slowly. Just a stolen kiss in the gardens. Come on. I'll show you."

"I can't wait." He'd been wanting to kiss her ever since they'd left the castle. Ever since the last time he'd kissed her. For seven long years.

Forever.

In one quick move, he pushed her into the shadows at the side of the arch and caged her against the stones. Her eyes darkened; her breath caught. He could have sworn he felt her body melting into his until every soft, round curve fit perfectly.

"Wait. In my fantasy, I'm supposed to be the seductress."

"You've done your job." He streaked his hands up her

sides and thrust his fingers into her hair and crushed her lips with his. The low purr in her throat shot fire straight to his loins. The desire he'd felt for her, already consuming, became even more raw, more impatient, more primitive. Undeniable. It beat in his blood, in his mind, until he couldn't think. He could only want. Take.

He inched them farther into the shadows, but she slowed his progress by fisting her hands in his hair to keep his mouth on hers. Gone was the slow, gentle seduction she'd begun beneath the arch. Her tongue met his, tangling, tasting, testing. Her hands were just as demanding, tugging his shirt free from his pants so she could run her hands up his back.

And those nails. Each scrape, each little stab fanned the flames she'd ignited with her story. He couldn't stop touching her. She was stronger than he'd imagined and more agile. She moved against him, not in submission but in aggression. *Give me more,* she seemed to demand. As if there were something he was holding back.

He wasn't. He couldn't. He thought he'd known all the variations of desire before, but it had never sliced at his control this way. As he dragged her closer, he thought that maybe she was all he'd ever wanted—the softness, the fire. When she was pressed against him like this, it was easy to block out the past, the future, and think only of now. Of having her right now.

Nell told herself she had to think. She had to breathe. But the searing heat he created was burning her seduction plans with the ferocity of a wildfire. When he tore away his mouth to run kisses over her face, her throat, she dragged in a breath and willed the oxygen to her brain. She needed a new plan.

"Wait."

"Nell…." His grip on her tightened. "You want me to stop?"

"No. I just want you to let me show you another fantasy I've dreamed of." The night air filled her lungs, and the sound of her ragged breathing mingled with his was erotic, tempting. "I've dreamed so often of doing this." She pulled his belt free. "And this." She unsnapped his jeans and tugged down the zipper. "And finally this." She freed him and wrapped her hand around him. The instant she did, she revised the rest of her plan because she simply couldn't wait another moment. "Now you can kiss me again."

The instant his mouth crushed hers, she did her best to melt into him. Her body had never felt this alive. She could even feel her blood racing through her veins. There was so much to absorb—every hard angle and plane of his body. The roughness of his hands as he gripped her hips to pull her closer. The sharp, unyielding press of the rocks at her back. Each separate sensation brought its own unique thrill.

He tore his mouth from hers to run his lips over her face as if he was determined to absorb every texture through the sense of taste alone. Then he kissed her again with a thorough, feverish fury as if he were looking for some flavor that she might deny him.

She denied him nothing. He was showing her more than anyone ever had, opening doors she hadn't known existed. And he could give her more. More than she'd ever imagined. The very thought that he might take her here and now, with such urgent need and desperation, sent her own desires spiraling. She raced her mouth down his neck, sank her teeth into the curve of his shoulder. The flavors were amazing. Addicting.

Now. The word hammered in her blood, pounded in her mind, as she dragged her mouth free of his. The cool night air eased her burning lungs as he dealt with her clothes. She thought she'd never felt anything more erotic than the slide of her dress over her arms and head. Once free of it, she wrapped her arms and legs around him.

They'd waited too long. A lifetime. He lifted her hips; she wrapped her legs around him.

"Now."

When she said the word, fresh needs exploded inside of him. Reid could see her eyes in the muted light, needed to see them as the last of his control shredded. He plunged into her. She surrounded him. For a moment, neither of them moved.

If he could have, he would have held on to the moment forever. But she'd weakened him when she'd begun to strip him. Unable to resist, he began to move, quickly, fiercely. The sultry sound of her moans fanned the flames as she matched him thrust for thrust until he knew nothing else, wanted nothing else. He swore once without knowing what he cursed. Then savagely he increased the pace. Faster and faster, harder and harder, they raced into the vortex of a storm—a place where neither of them had ever been. Then they shattered.

SANITY SLIPPED IN SLOWLY. Reid had no idea how long he'd stood there, pressing her into the stone arch as bits and pieces of reality trickled in. She was still wrapped tightly around him, her head on his shoulder. His breath was still coming in gasps. His heart was still hammering against his chest. He still couldn't think clearly.

And he was trembling.

No woman had ever made him tremble before. Somehow he found the strength to angle his head so that he could look at her. Her eyes were open, dazed. A fresh wave of desire shot through him. He felt himself grow hard again inside her.

Good Lord, he needed a moment. Just a moment, he told himself. Or he was going to take her again like a madman.

Murmuring his name, Nell ran her hand down his back. There'd been something in his eyes when he'd looked at her—vulnerability. It had her nestling closer. The gesture flooded him with warmth.

"It wasn't exactly what I'd planned."

"I'll take it. Gladly." Reid tipped her chin up. "Are you all right? I wasn't careful."

She smiled at him. "Neither was I."

"I wasn't careful about something else. Protection."

She cupped his face in her hands. "I have it covered."

His body jerked, pressing her hard into the side of the arch. The pinging sound registered in her brain at the same instant that she felt the sting on her cheek. Reid pivoted, holding her tightly against him as he sprinted into the stone arch. Then she was on the ground, his body on top of hers and her breath whooshed out.

"Don't move," he said.

Not a possibility. She could barely drag in a breath. Her mind was racing to process what had just happened—the jerk of Reid's body, the sound like stone hitting stone.

"What happened?" she asked.

"Someone took a shot at us." He'd lifted his head and was staring beyond them through the other end of the tunnel at the wooded hillside behind the stone arch. Her lover was gone and the Secret Service agent was back.

"The floodlights don't spill in this far," he was saying, "so I think we're safe for the moment. Stay put."

When he moved, she gripped his shoulders and held tight. "You shouldn't leave again. You said we were safe here."

"Cell phone," he said. "I'm calling Daryl. He can douse the floodlights."

That was when she realized that her hand was wet. Sticky. When she saw the dark color, fear fluttered in her throat like a trapped bird. "He...hit you."

"A scratch." Without bothering to check the wound, he spoke into his cell. "Daryl, we've got a problem. We're in the stone arch. Someone took a shot at us a couple of seconds ago. He nicked my upper arm, but Nell's fine. I figure the shooter was in the hills behind the arch. About twenty-five feet up and maybe fifty feet to the right."

The floodlights went out.

"Thanks. We were beneath the stones for five to ten minutes, and when we stepped out, we lingered at the side of the arch for a minute or so."

Lingered.

She could only seem to process one word at a time. From the moment she'd felt Reid's blood, it was as if her brain had been frozen. As he outlined to Daryl what had happened, reality sank in. While they'd made love, someone—a sniper—had taken aim at Reid and shot him.

A wave of dizziness struck her.

They'd lingered.

To fulfill her fantasy. Her fault. They'd made love

right out in the open when someone was threatening to kill off her family. And Reid. Her fault again. She tightened her grip on him and held on for dear life.

"Relax," he murmured, pulling off her hands. Then he shifted so that he could keep an eye on both entrances. "Daryl will be here in a moment, and we'll get you safely back to the castle."

But it wasn't *her* safety that had been threatened. She'd put her subplot in front of her plot, and it had nearly cost Reid his life.

10

"WHOEVER IT WAS, they're a damn good shot." Daryl studied the extra whiteboard he'd dragged into the main parlor from Adair's office. On it he'd sketched the clearing, the stone arch and the hillside beyond. He pointed to the place where he thought the sniper had taken his shot. "I bet he was standing right here."

Reid's mind flashed back to the instant he'd felt the fiery sensation sear the side of his shoulder. He remembered that, and the icy stab of fear that had pierced right to his core—and then nothing until he was standing by Nell midway beneath the stone arch. Even now, he had no recollection of how he'd gotten her there.

That was a first for him. He took a sip of the brandy Daryl had poured him after Vi had tended to the scratch the bullet had left.

A bullet meant for Nell.

In the bright lights of the kitchen with Vi and Nell, he'd seen how tired Nell had looked. There'd been dark circles beneath her eyes, and for the first time he'd glimpsed fear in them. His fault. He'd never treated a woman with less care. And he'd never been this careless on a job.

Vi had agreed with his assessment of Nell's exhaustion, because she'd hurried her niece upstairs, so that she could shower and change and get some rest. The dog had gone with the women.

In the parlor, Daryl drew his finger down to where he'd sketched the stone arch. "If you were here, you would have been out of range of the floodlights. I'll bet he was wearing night vision goggles."

"Which means he's either a pro or he's had military training," Reid said.

"Agreed."

Reid wanted badly to pace off his nerves. Another first for him. He never paced.

"While Vi was patching you up, I updated Sheriff Skinner. He's got a man stationed there right now to guard the area."

"At first light, I want to search for the bullet."

Daryl met his eyes. "My thoughts exactly. It might shed some light on who we're dealing with." Then he tapped on the sketch again. "By then, Skinner will have volunteers patrolling the hillside and searching for any casing. He said he'd have no trouble getting the manpower. Edie's a popular woman in Glen Loch, and no one wants trouble at her granddaughter's wedding rehearsal. Everyone in town's grateful for the economic boost that this wedding business has given the local community."

"Nell is not going to want to stay inside the castle," Reid said. "She's determined to find the necklace, and I'm worried about the number of strangers who will be here tomorrow."

"With the extra manpower Skinner is mustering up, we ought to be able to handle it. I'll print up copies of the police artist's sketch that Duncan sent us so Skinner can distribute them to his volunteers. Not that it will help much since he was wearing sunglasses and a beard. That reporter from the *Times* will be here at ten to interview Vi and shadow her for the rest of the day. I'll stick with them. Vi has two appointments with prospective clients, and the wedding rehearsal starts at four. That will involve less than a dozen people, and none of them will be strangers. I'll also have a man at my office check more deeply into Gwendolen Campbell's known acquaintances. He can take another look at Deanna Lewis's circle. Someone with a military background might pop up."

Reid could hear the clock ticking in his head. "I never should have agreed to take her out there tonight. I let her convince me that they wouldn't want to eliminate her until she'd found the necklace. I've never been this off my game."

Daryl turned to him. "You're not off your game. The shooter didn't want to hit Nell. He wanted to hit you."

Reid stared at him. The man was right. And he should have realized it sooner. He was definitely off his game. That had to stop.

"What did we miss?" Nell asked as she and Vi joined them.

"You should be in bed," Reid said.

"Save your breath," Vi said. "I lost that argument ten minutes ago."

"I was just telling Reid that he was the shooter's target and not you," Daryl said.

"I know," Nell said. "It's my fault for convincing Reid to go out there."

"No." Reid waited until she met his gaze. "I'm responsible for what happened, and I'm going to make sure it doesn't happen again."

Nell felt a band tighten around her heart. He was talking about more than the shooter, and he was right. Hadn't she already realized that she had to modify her subplot? She couldn't, she wouldn't put him in danger again. If that meant she had to put her garden fantasy on hold until she'd figured out where Eleanor had hidden her necklace, she could live with that. She'd waited seven years. She could certainly wait to seduce him in the garden until after sundown tomorrow. If all went well, she'd find the necklace by then.

At least that was the argument she'd made to herself when she had been in the shower.

So why did it hurt so much that he'd come to the same conclusion?

"The person responsible for all this is the person who thinks they have a right to Eleanor's sapphires," Vi said as she urged Nell toward sofa. "The best way to put an end to it is to catch them."

Daryl poured two brandies and handed them to the women. "Reid and I agree that the shooter is either a professional or perhaps ex-military."

"What if it's someone who shoots for sport?" Nell asked. "Gwendolen and Deanna are both from Great Britain. Perhaps they hunt or skeet shoot. Obviously Deanna couldn't have been out there on the hillside tonight, but Gwendolen could."

The two men exchanged a look. "Nell could be

right," Daryl said. "I'll have my man check it out." Then he turned to Nell. "How did you think of that?"

"The characters I create for my stories all have backgrounds, and we've pretty much established that the villains in this case have a connection to Eleanor and Angus that reaches back to Scotland." She smiled at Daryl. "Plus hunting and skeet shooting are big on British television."

"Reid tells me that you think the clue to the location of Eleanor's necklace is in the painting," Daryl said.

Nell moved so she could stand directly beneath the portrait. As she passed the second whiteboard that Daryl had used to sketch out the time line of events, she gave it a glance and once more experienced that little tug on her memory that she'd experienced earlier in the evening, but whatever was lingering at the edge of her mind stayed there. Shifting her gaze to Eleanor, she tried to focus.

Finding the necklace had to be at the top of her priority list. "She was so careful hiding the two earrings. She wanted them to be eventually found. So she had to have left clues."

"Cam is sure that's why someone was paying those nocturnal visits to our library six months ago," Vi said. "Trying to find those clues before Adair found the first earring."

"The stone arch is definitely in the portrait," Daryl said. "But what about the cave in the cliff face where Duncan and Piper found the second earring?"

He was right, Nell thought with a sinking heart. In the beats of silence that followed Daryl's comment, she waited for Reid to say something. Anything. When he didn't, the little band of pain tightened around her heart.

The necklace, she lectured herself. Plot before subplot. But no matter how hard she stared at the portrait, she couldn't make the cliffs appear. If Eleanor was seated in the gazebo as her father had always insisted she was, there was no way to fit the cliffs in the background.

"If she left the jewels behind in different places, maybe she didn't feel the need to put the clues all in the portrait," Vi said. "Maybe that's why our nighttime visitor spent so much time in the library."

No one said a word, but Nell was sure they were all thinking the same thing. If there was a clue in the library, discovering it would be like finding a needle in a haystack. Someone had spent six months working there and had come up empty.

A wave of exhaustion suddenly hit Nell. An arm went around her shoulders. Not Reid's but her aunt Vi's.

"We need to sleep on it," Vi said as she drew Nell toward the door. "Let our subconscious minds sort through it. Things will be better in the morning."

They'd better be, Nell thought. Then she remembered the notes she'd tucked into her fantasy box, and her tiredness began to fade. She was going to find Eleanor's necklace by sundown tomorrow.

And she was going to seduce Reid Sutherland tonight, just not in the garden. Yet.

REID STOOD ON the balcony of his room, his hands gripping the stone railing like a lifeline. He'd stepped out because it was as far away as he could get from the connecting door to Nell's bedroom. The cold shower he'd already taken hadn't done a thing to lessen his desire. While the water had poured down on him, he had reviewed the reasons why it would be a mistake to go to her. She needed sleep badly. He needed some distance to regain his perspective. Making love to her again would only increase her expectation that he could give her something that he was incapable of. He didn't want to hurt her more than he already had. Etcetera, etcetera and so forth.

Cut the crap, Sutherland. The real reason you're holding on to the railing like a lifeline is because you want more than to make love to her again. You simply want to be with her. To lie beside her and hold her. To talk to her. Not just about the case or the sapphires. He wanted to know more about her. What she'd shared with him beneath the stone arch had only made him more curious.

Pillow talk. It was an old-fashioned and clichéd term that his mother had used to describe one of the joys of her marriage to A.D. The fact that he could envision himself doing it with Nell scared the hell out of him. Spending the night with a woman had been near the top of his never-do list. He'd never brought one to his home because he valued the freedom, the flexibility to leave before morning. Staying the night built the kind of intimacy he'd never desired.

With Nell, he wanted to spend the night, to wake in the morning holding her close, to see her face in the light of a new day. He wanted intimacy.

Damn her. No other woman had made him want more than he could have.

Lifting his hands from the stone railing, he found that his fingers had gone numb from the tightness of his grip. He had to think of something else. Vi had been right. He needed to sleep. While he slept, perhaps his unconscious mind would let him know what to do about Nell.

But the thought of going to an empty bed kept him lingering on the balcony. The night was so quiet that he could hear individual waves licking the rocks along the shore. Flexing his fingers, he shifted his focus to the gardens that stretched from beneath his balcony to the stone arch and the hillside in one direction and the lake in the other.

The stone arch was clearly visible in the floodlights, and the moon spilled enough light to make out the tops of the trees and the shadowy paths that wound through the gardens. Nell was so sure that Eleanor had left clues in the painting, but Daryl had been dead-on. The cliff face was on the opposite side of the castle from the gardens. If Eleanor had intended to leave clues to the location of the sapphires in the painting, she'd left a big one out.

And if he stayed on his balcony all night, he definitely wouldn't be at the top of his game tomorrow. He was about to turn and head for bed when his cell phone rang. A quick glance at the caller ID told him that it was Cam. He must have news.

"Problem or favor?" Reid asked.

"Neither. Adair and I discovered something...curious."

Reid knew his brother well enough—Cam wouldn't call in the middle of the night unless he thought it was important. Aware of how sound could carry over water, he stepped back into his bedroom and slid the balcony doors shut. "Tell me."

"It was Adair's idea," Cam said. "Mom's been in the library ever since she got permission to visit the Campbell estate, and A.D.'s been in the gardens. Neither one of them has gotten a tour of the castle, so this afternoon Adair convinced the housekeeper to give us one."

"You found something on our Gwendolen," Reid said.

"Not exactly. We learned the estate has fallen on hard times. The story in the village is that it started to decline about two hundred years ago—just about the time of Angus and Eleanor's flight to the New World. Due to the lack of a male heir in Eleanor's generation, the castle and the estate went to a cousin, but the money just wasn't there. The present housekeeper says that her mother worked here after the Second World War when most of the furniture was sold or taken by debt collectors. She's still alive, and we're going to visit her first thing in the morning. But it's what we didn't find on our tour that's curious."

"What did you not find on your tour?"

"About the only things that didn't get sold are a series of portraits in the upstairs ballroom. It's a regular rogues' gallery of Campbell heirs and family members. Each generation has a family portrait with the male heir and his wife and children. The last one has Eleanor in it—the same long blond hair. The housekeeper says the family wouldn't sell them, but it's more likely that the pictures wouldn't be of much value to anyone but the Campbells."

It was unlike Cam to take so long in getting to the point, and that fact alone had Reid's curiosity growing.

"The thing is, none of the wives are wearing the sapphires—not even Eleanor's mother," he said. "Adair's been nagging me ever since we left the ballroom to call you about it. She says that the sapphires should be in the paintings, and she claims their conspicuous absence means that Deanna Lewis might be right. The sapphires were not Eleanor's dowry because they never belonged to the Campbells."

"There's certainly an argument to be made for that theory," Reid said. In his mind he could hear Nell making it. If the Campbells had been in legitimate possession of the Stuart sapphires, surely a record would have been displayed in the family portraits.

"Yeah," Cam said in a resigned tone. "It opens up a whole new can of worms. If the Stuart sapphires didn't belong to the Campbells, who the hell did they belong to and how did Eleanor get hold of them?"

"That's what you need to find out. And fast," Reid said. "Anything else?"

"Now that you mention it, I am curious about whether or not you've read the fantasies in the MacPherson sisters' fantasy box."

Reid let a beat of silence go by. Of course, Cam would know about the box. Duncan would probably know about it, also. "No, I haven't."

"Well, you have a treat in store. Long story short, the sisters got together on the night our parents married and wrote some very explicit sexual fantasies. Then they buried them in the stone arch so that they would eventually come true. Nell wrote hers on pink paper, and it's very interesting."

Reid frowned. "Are you telling me that you've read them?"

"Hey, I'm CIA. I'm trained to leave no stone unturned."

Reid couldn't identify all the emotions that shot through him. Fury that someone had invaded Nell's privacy was the first one. "You had no business reading Nell's."

"Whoa, big bro. Calm down."

Reid was shocked to find that he needed to. He was pacing, and his free hand had clenched into a fist. If Cam had been in the room, that fist would already have collided with his jaw. He stopped short and drew in a deep breath.

"You're in love with her, aren't you?" Cam asked.

Reid found he couldn't answer. He was very much afraid that the answer was yes. And if he said it out loud…

"I'm going to take your silence as an affirmation," Cam said. "I bet Duncan that you'd be a goner within the first twelve hours of your arrival at the castle. The profiler believes that you're a cautious man, and it would take at least twenty-four hours for you to take the fall. I win." Cam was chuckling as he ended the call.

Reid stood there for a moment staring down at his cell phone. Then he reached deep for his control. He couldn't, he wouldn't think about his feelings for Nell right now. He had a forty-eight-hour countdown clock to deal with, which left them only thirty-six hours at most. When he glanced up, he discovered he was standing right in front of the connecting door to Nell's room, his hand on the knob. But before he could turn it, it opened, and he barely recognized this version of Nell, who took one of his hands and drew him into her room.

11

NELL'S HEART THREATENED to pound right out of her chest. She was not going to let Reid spoil her plan this time. Not after all her careful preparations.

He'd taken forever to get to his room. She'd used the time to light candles, chill champagne and dress in the black lace designer lingerie she'd purchased in the boutique below Piper's apartment. When she'd put it on and looked at herself in the mirror, she hadn't even recognized the old Nell.

Perfect. The lacy tank top stopped just short of the string-bikini-style panties, leaving the skin at her waist exposed. She placed a hand there now to help her focus.

It wasn't just black lace that she'd armed herself with. She also had plenty of other ideas. But there was a world of difference between imagining something and actually doing it. In her daydreams she'd never had to deal with the effect of his gaze as it swept down her body. Flames licked first along the nerve endings at her throat, then flickered lower to the sensitive skin at the tops of her breasts. She sucked in a breath when she felt the fire reach her belly, then sear her legs right down to her toes. He was still fully clothed, and that made her remember her plan.

Strip him. You can definitely do that. Just talk your way through it.

Careful not to look directly into his eyes or at his mouth, she said, "I intend to seduce you, Reid. I wanted to do it in the gardens, but it may be a while before either of us is safe there."

Good. Words had always come easily to her.

"You have too many clothes on." She reached for the first button on his shirt and slipped it free. "Better."

She could do this.

"Nell—"

"Shh." Tamping down on the impulse to meet his eyes, she concentrated on the second button and felt a spurt of triumph when she freed it. "You don't have to say a word. You want to tell me that we both need our sleep if we're going to find the necklace tomorrow. And you're expecting that I'll obey like the good little girl I was at six. But I'm not that girl anymore."

As if to emphasize her point to both of them, she ignored the last button, and in a move she'd dreamed of forever, she shoved the shirt down his arms so that it trapped his wrists at his sides. When he sucked in his breath, the thrill shot straight through her.

Turning him, she placed a hand on his chest and urged him toward her bed. "Do you know how long I've dreamed of getting you out of your clothes?" The fast thud of his heart against her palm was rewarding, arousing. When she backed him into the side of the mattress, she slid her hand down his now-bare chest to his belt. Thrilled at his quick expulsion of breath, she lingered there, tracing her finger along the top of his waistband.

"I wanted to do this on the day our parents were married." Taking her time, she unfastened the buckle, then pulled the belt through the loops. Slowly. "I described the way I would strip you in one of the fantasies I wrote about you that night."

Moonlight streamed through the glass doors, highlighting all the planes and angles of the skin she'd exposed. She simply had to touch him again. Tossing the belt aside, she ran her hands from his waist to his throat. It wasn't just the sight of him that fascinated her. She loved the contrast in their skin tones. His was tan; hers was pale. Pleasure sharpened at each response. The sound of his breath expelling when her nails scraped down over his nipples, the rapid hammer of his heart against her lips, the way her name caught in his throat when she unsnapped his jeans and slid the zipper down—each separate sensation thrilled her, enchanted her.

"Nell…"

The desperation in his tone was contagious. And it was all so incredibly good. Glorious. How had she managed to wait for so long? His hands rested on her shoulders, but without the strength that she'd felt before. Her confidence surged. "There's more." Impatient now, she shoved his jeans down over his hips.

And there *was* more.

Her gaze froze on silky black jockeys. The material was sheer and revealing. "I never imagined the full impact of being with you."

How could she? At eighteen, her experience had been limited. Now, she realized, it still was. There'd been no time to see him during that firestorm of desire at the side of the stone arch. No time to touch him. Craving tore at her. She'd take the time now.

"Nice," she murmured as she danced her fingers down the length of him.

"Nell…"

The word came out on a moan, delighting her and encouraging her to press her hand more firmly against him. "Very sexy. And we're so compatible. Who would have thought?"

Because her mind had begun to spin, she was having trouble thinking at all. She couldn't stop touching him. Was it her imagination or had he grown even harder as she stroked her fingers up and down the length of him? "This… You…go beyond anything I dreamed of."

Her hands moved of their own accord, her fingers slipping beneath the waistband of his briefs. "I wrote about doing this.

"And this."

When she dropped to her knees and began to use her mouth on him, Reid slid his fingers from her shoulders into her hair and held on. Helpless. That's what she'd made him. The sensation skittered in his stomach, melted his muscles, burned through his brain. He should tell her to stop. But if he could have spoken, he would have begged her to continue on. And he'd never begged a woman before. He'd never wanted one so desperately.

The sensations she brought with a flick of her tongue, the soft wet caress of her mouth, the scrape of her teeth steeped him in pleasures he'd never known. Agonizing. Outrageous. Magnificent. He'd never allowed another woman to seduce him. He'd never been willing to hand over the reins of control.

With Nell he hadn't had a choice. She'd cast a spell

on him from the moment that he'd opened the door to her room and seen her standing there in those scraps of black lace. He'd literally ached for her, and that had stunned him as nothing else ever had.

People were only turned to stone in legends and myths—or in the Bible. That kind of thing didn't happen in real life. And certainly not to him.

Until that moment she'd opened the connecting door. Since then, he hadn't been able to move or think or say anything but her name since. He couldn't seem to talk at all now. Nor could he stop her when she rose and pushed him back on the bed.

Everything about her bewitched him. As she climbed onto the mattress and straddled him, he wanted to reach for her, but the weakness in his limbs persisted. She'd trapped him in a world of pleasure, a world where her goal seemed to be to fulfill every desire he'd ever had. All he could see was her face above him. The play of moonlight in her hair shifted the color from pale gold to silver. When her mouth hovered over his, when their breaths mingled, he said, "I want you, Nell."

"Soon." Her lips brushed his, then she linked their fingers and pressed his hands into the mattress. "You should relax. I'm just getting started."

"Kiss me."

"My pleasure." She was careful to avoid his mouth, nipping his chin instead. As she took her lips on a slow journey along his jaw, down his throat and across his shoulder, she absorbed the sound of his ragged breathing. She lingered at the bandage, kissing it softly.

"I've fantasized so often about tasting you." Inch by inch, she moved her mouth down his chest, licking here, nipping there. "So many flavors." She took his nipple into her mouth and suckled. Then, shifting her body downward, she delighted in the rich dark taste beneath his pecs and in the rapid beating of his heart against her lips.

Even in her wildest fantasies she hadn't anticipated the thrill she experienced when the hairs on his chest brushed against her own nipples or the excitement when his fingers went lax in hers. Lost in him now, she moved lower, exploring his body with her mouth alone.

When she slid her tongue into his navel, his fingers gripped hers hard. "Nell…"

She raised her head, met his eyes and what she saw ignited a flame that threatened to melt her. She tried to refocus on her plan. "I'm still just getting started. I poured some champagne, and I have so many ideas."

As she wiggled up his body and lifted the glass from a bedside table, a shock wave of heat melted his bones, his will. Through a haze of desire, he watched her dip her fingers into the flute. When the cold drops hit his face, his lips, his neck, they sent a blast of fire right to his core. Even though his hands were free now, he couldn't seem to lift them, didn't want to.

She leaned down and began to lick at his lips. "Mmm. You taste even better mixed with champagne." She traced her tongue over his mouth. "Delicious."

Then she sprinkled his chest with champagne and took her mouth on the same journey as before. Reid found himself totally trapped in a world of ice and fire. Tremors danced along his skin. A searing heat shot through his body. The sounds of pleasure she made as she used her mouth on him vibrated through his system and smoked through his brain.

She was devouring him as if he were some rare treat

that she'd waited all her life to sample. Just as he'd waited all his life for her.

He had to have more. Gripping her shoulders, he drew her up so that she met his eyes.

"I have more ideas," she said with a smile.

"So do I," he said as he hooked an arm around her and shifted her beneath him on the mattress. "Let me show you."

His intention had been to go slowly, to mimic the method she'd used on him. But the instant he pressed his mouth to hers, he felt his control stretch to the breaking point. At the first possessive sweep of his hands, her response tore through him. She arched against him, demanding more, as if there were something he was holding back. He wasn't. He couldn't.

They rolled across the bed as if they were combatants instead of lovers. As soon as he could, Reid tore at the silk that still covered her breast, then used his mouth on the skin he exposed inch by inch by inch. Any thought he might have had of savoring the rich, ripe taste of her skin vanished in a savage attack of hunger.

More.

He wasn't sure who said the word or if he'd only thought it. But everywhere he touched, everywhere he tasted, she showed him more, enchanting him all over again. Her scent was lightest at her wrist, heavier at her throat and addicting beneath her breast. She was generous beyond any man's fantasy. But each sigh, each shiver, each scrape of her nails or nip of her teeth left him wanting more. And more.

So he took. And took. Though he had no idea how, they were now in his bedroom, on the floor in a pool of moonlight when she finally rose above him. She filled his vision. Her skin was sheened with moisture, her eyes filled with his reflection. He tried to say her name, but the air burned so fiercely in his lungs that it came out on a gasp. Guiding her hips, he plunged into her, felt her close around him, and once more he felt as if she'd turned him to stone.

He wanted more than anything to hold on to the moment—to make time spin out. To hold them both there on that delicious, dangerous edge where she belonged only to him.

She moved first, arching on top of him, and he watched her eyes as her pleasure built and peaked. Even as her climax abated, he held himself still, determined to extend the moment when she thought only of him. Then her eyes cleared, and she began to move again. "More."

His control snapped as did any grasp he had on civilized matters. *Mine.* It was the only word he could think of as he thrust into her again and again. But as pleasure exploded and sent them both shooting over the edge, he poured more and more of himself into her. The last word he thought of was *hers.*

NELL MOVED IN a dream world where mists swirled, thickening in some places, thinning in others. She tried to wake up, but couldn't seem to break free. Her limbs felt heavy as if she were walking through water. The strange sensation should have frightened her, but all she felt was a burning curiosity. She searched for some sign of where she was.

Nothing.

With her vision totally impaired, she concentrated on her other senses. She smelled wood burning, heard it snap and crackle, and there was music—a tune she didn't recognize from an instrument she thought she did.

Bagpipes?

As the sound grew stronger, the mist thinned enough for her to make out the silhouette of a couple dancing. Over their heads, candles flickered in crystal chandeliers. At the far end of the room, a fire roared in a huge hearth. There were other people in the room, but they stood in the shadows watching and whispering as the man and woman turned this way and that, moving gracefully to the music.

It was like a fairy tale, Nell thought. She might have been witnessing Prince Charming and Cinderella dancing at the ball—a Disney movie come to life. Except the woman was familiar.

Though she could only see her back, Nell was certain she'd seen her before. Her frame was slender. Blond hair tumbled in loose curls below her shoulders. When her partner turned her, candles struck brilliance into the sapphires that dangled from her ears and nestled at her throat, and recognition had Nell's heart taking a leap.

Eleanor.

She was younger than the woman in the portrait and even more beautiful. When the music had the couple turning again, Nell caught a quick glimpse of the man's face. He was much taller than Eleanor, his hair dark, his features handsome. He turned again, giving Nell a second look.

Not Angus. He bore no resemblance to the likenesses that remained of her several-times-great-grandfather. Still, he too was familiar. Nell was certain she knew him.

She had to get a better look, but before she could move, the mists descended, blanketing the scene in front of her with the finality of a curtain falling on the final act. The air chilled. Gone was the scent of burning wood and the music. She smelled jasmine and roses now, and the only sound piercing the silence came from a breeze rushing through the trees.

Nell felt a surge of urgency as she pushed her way forward. There was something more she had to see. She was sure of it. When the mist finally abated, she recognized the stone arch immediately. Beneath it stood a couple. The man's back was to her, but Eleanor was bathed in moonlight. She wore the same white dress she'd danced in, and the sapphires gleamed bright at her throat and ears. But her expression was troubled. Then the man lifted her off her feet, pressed her close and kissed her.

Eleanor kissed him back, wrapping her arms around him and holding on for dear life. Though she hadn't been aware of moving, Nell realized that she was closer now. The couple stood in profile, and Nell saw that the man kissing Eleanor was Angus and not the man she'd been dancing with. But even as the certainty of that flashed through her, the mists swirled in, thick and gray.

This time when they cleared, her vision remained blurred. The image in front of her took form slowly, one detail at a time. She was still standing in front of the stone arch. And there was still a couple beneath it. But it wasn't Angus and Eleanor who stood so close they might have been one.

The man was Reid. And she was the woman he was kissing. She knew because she felt the searing brand of his mouth pressed to hers, and she felt her own response break free and wild. She tightened her grip on him and let the mists sweep them away.

12

THE EASTERN SKY was barely pink with the promise of the sun when Skinner had pulled into the driveway just as he and Daryl had stepped into the clearing in front of the stone arch. Reid had filled them in on what Cam and Adair had discovered in Scotland. Reid split up from Sheriff Skinner and Daryl to begin searching for the bullet that had grazed his shoulder the night before.

When they'd left the castle, Vi had been in the kitchen making scones, and even though he knew the two women were perfectly safe, he'd asked Vi to take Alba up to Nell's room to guard her.

Better to be doubly safe than sorry. Better still to find something that might identify the shooter who'd aimed a bullet at him. The hills on this side of the castle kept the area around the stone arch blanketed in shadows, adding an extra challenge to the job. Moments earlier Daryl had suggested they divide the area into three concentric half circles.

Chances were good that the bullet had ricocheted off the stones, so Skinner was looking in the outermost half circle, ten yards out; Daryl was examining every inch of the middle one, five yards out; and then Reid was searching the area closest to the arch itself. If they didn't find it, they'd widen the search area.

He ran his hand over the stones at eye level where he estimated he and Nell had been standing the night before, and he felt his fingers brush against the coolness of steel. Stepping back, he took out his penknife and used the flashlight at the end of it. The glint of metal was unmistakable. Seconds later, he'd managed to free it from the rocks. Keeping his voice stage-whisper low, he said, "I've got it."

Daryl reached him with Skinner two steps behind. Reid passed the bullet to Daryl first. For a few moments, there were only the sounds of the gentle lapping of the water in the distance and the chirping of morning birds.

"Nothing I recognize on sight," Daryl said. "That pretty much eliminates most of what the military is using as well as what the pros are favoring. My office can get a lab in Albany to take a look at it, but that will take time. Overnighting it to my office in D.C. might get us quicker results."

But not quick enough. Reid heard the clock ticking in his head. The sound had been there since he'd awakened, beating in rhythm to the pumping of his blood.

"Benjy Grimshaw might be able to help us out," Sheriff Skinner said. "He's the father of the bride, and he manages the sporting goods department at our general store. Guns have always been his hobby. His grandson helps him with his blog, and a lot of collectors visit his site."

Reid met Daryl's gaze. "We might as well have him take a look before we send it anywhere."

When Daryl handed him the bullet, Skinner said,

"If my men find a casing up there in the hills, I'll send that along to Benjy, too."

"If you've got a minute, I'd like to run over the schedule for the wedding rehearsal with you," Daryl said. "When Reid and I left the kitchen, Vi was putting a tray of scones into the oven."

Skinner's smile spread slowly. "You've just successfully bribed an officer of the law."

"Save one for me," Reid said. "I'm going to take a short detour over to the old gazebo. Nell's going to want to pay it a visit, and I need to check out what I'm up against in terms of security."

Daryl stopped and looked at Reid. "You should be safe enough right now with the sheriff's volunteers up in the hills. But no promises on the scones."

"I'll have to rely on my prodigal son status." Reid shot Daryl a smile before he veered off on a path that led deeper into the gardens. He wanted to visit the gazebo alone, and Daryl had been astute enough to realize that. Cam was a lucky man to have Daryl for a boss. Reid hoped he'd be half as lucky finding the ruins of the old gazebo. He'd been ten the last time he was there.

The hedges lining the path rose high enough in places to mimic a maze, preventing him from having a clear view of where he was going. And providing too damn many places to hide. Relying on instinct, Reid angled his way to the left of the stone arch and closer to the lake.

He'd told Daryl the truth. He did need to check out any security problems. But that wasn't the only reason he wanted some time by himself. If he went back to the castle right now, he wasn't sure Vi's scones could prevent him from going back to Nell.

When he'd awakened, her head had been tucked in the crook of his shoulder, and he hadn't been able to take his eyes off her. In the thin rays of morning light slipping through the drapes of his bedroom, she'd looked outrageously beautiful. The pale gold hair and porcelain skin made her appear fragile and delicate. But he'd learned her strength, experienced the passion of those frantic hands, those wild lips. During the night, she'd seduced him the way any man dreamed of being seduced, and layer by layer she'd stripped him of any claim he had on sanity. More, she'd unlocked a place inside him that he hadn't even known was there, and for a moment he'd glimpsed what his life might be like if he could wake every morning with his arms wrapped around her.

It was fear that had galvanized him enough to get out of bed. But he wasn't sure what he was more afraid of—the new desire he'd discovered in himself or the possibility of it being denied?

And what did Nell want?

What she'd told him or something else?

And where were the ruins of the old gazebo? He was certain he'd gone too far and was about to retrace his steps, when he spotted the rubble through a narrow break in the hedge. At first glance, the area looked as though it had been abandoned for a long time. Flowers grew everywhere, poking through rocks and at times totally obscuring what appeared to be a low circular wall of stones. The circle was uneven, and there were breaks where it totally disappeared. But Reid knew that, with a little digging, he would find stones beneath the earth that had covered them over time.

When he'd completed a walk around the perimeter,

he was sure of three things. Though there were many more flowers than he recalled, this was the place that Nell had brought him on that long-ago summer day. He could even identify the exact spot where she'd invited him to sit and drink tea.

There was no sign left of the wooden latticework or even what had been the floor of the structure. But Reid would have staked money on A.D.'s theory that this was where the gazebo in the portrait had once stood.

Allowing Nell to linger here for any length of time would be dangerous. He swept his gaze along the top of the hedge. Anyone approaching would be totally blocked from view, and there were areas where someone could see in, just as he had. A hedge would provide no protection from a bullet.

Reid ignored the icy fear that slithered up his spine. He needed a cool head. His best option would be to refuse to let her come here. Since that had no chance in hell of flying, he'd have to go with option two. Minimize the risk, and that always had to do with timing. Three years of heading up security for a vice president who disliked playing it safe was going to come in handy again. The trick would be to bring her here when the visitors to the castle were at a minimum, and to get her in and out as quickly as possible.

Quickly reviewing the schedule in his head, Reid calculated that perfect window of opportunity for Nell's visit to the old gazebo would be while the reporter from the *Times* was interviewing and shadowing Vi. James Orbison was scheduled to arrive in less than two hours. That meant Nell could sleep for a while longer. Then Daryl could keep his eyes on the writer and Vi, while

Reid and Nell tried to uncover what Eleanor wanted them to see in the place she'd chosen for her portrait.

He swept his gaze around the area again.

Carefully making his way into the center of the circle, he wished for a step stool. The hedges surrounding the area were high enough to block any view he might have of the stone arch. He figured the floor of the gazebo would have been level with the top of his thigh, the bench Eleanor was sitting on even higher. From that vantage point, the stone arch would have been clearly visible to anyone in the gazebo. And so would the south facade of the castle and the cliffs beyond.

It should take about fifteen seconds for Nell to figure that out. But he knew her well enough now that she'd want to linger a bit longer. In fact…chances were good that this had been the destination she'd had in mind last night. *The gardens.* She'd wanted to seduce him right here.

Was that all she wanted? Just a few days of indulgence—and then they'd go on their separate ways? That's what she'd said, and the words had perfectly matched his own desires. Or so he'd thought.

Frowning, he looked in the direction of the stone arch. There was one way to find out exactly what she wanted. Cam had claimed she'd written her desires down in explicit detail. As Reid pushed his way through the hedge and headed toward the arch, he wondered if reading her fantasies had been his goal from the moment he'd stepped out of the castle this morning.

NELL WOKE UP as she always did with her sensory perceptions just a few seconds ahead of her mind and her feelings. Her view of the ceiling told her that she was at the castle. But not in her own bed.

Because she'd finally seduced Reid.

The memory rushed in along with delight and triumph. And joy. She wanted to savor what had happened, celebrate it and relive each detail, but a jingling bell had her sitting straight up in bed. Alba rose from her prone position in front of the door and padded to her side.

That's when it sank in. "Reid's gone." The tightening around Nell's heart had her pressing the heel of her hand against her chest. She noted the indentation in the pillow, but when she explored it with her hand, it was cold.

"He left you here to do the bodyguard work," she said to Alba.

Why did that hurt so much? Disappointment she could understand. If Reid had been here, she would have seduced him again. Happily.

But what she was feeling cut deeper. She wanted him here. Needed him here.

"Loss," she murmured as she patted the bed so that the dog would join her. Alba jumped up, circled once and settled next to Nell's thigh.

"I suppose that, since you came from a shelter, you've experienced your share of rejection," Nell said. "But I've been lucky." She scratched Alba behind the ears. "There was that cad I thought I was in love with in college. He told me that he loved me, and I believed him. Everyone has always loved me, so I was sucker enough to believe him. Once I went to bed with him, I found out that I was just one more notch on his belt. Classic story."

Alba plopped her head on Nell's lap.

She frowned. "It's absolutely unreasonable that this

hurts more." It wasn't as though he'd left her. He took his job as bodyguard too seriously. The dog was proof of that.

To confirm her suspicion, she grabbed the sheet, wrapping it around herself as she hurried to the sliding glass doors. Even as she slid them open, she spotted Reid sitting with Daryl at the far end of the kitchen terrace. "See," she murmured to the dog who'd joined her. "From where he's sitting, he can keep an eye on all the balconies on this side of the castle. The perfect Secret Service vantage point."

Was that all she was to him? A job? When she caught herself rubbing her chest again, she jerked her hand away and frowned down at it. "There's no reason to feel bad because he left me with you." She hadn't lost Reid.

Yet.

The band around her heart tightened even more—because she would lose him. Hadn't she explained it very clearly to him? Once they found Eleanor's necklace and everyone was safe, she and Reid would go their separate ways. Seduction had been the plan, not a lifelong commitment. If she wanted that, all she would have had to do was follow her aunt's advice and kiss him beneath the stones.

Panic replaced the tight feeling around her heart as she remembered doing just that.

In a dream, she reminded herself. It had all been a strange dream that had started out with Eleanor dancing with another man and ended when Eleanor had kissed Angus beneath the stones.

And then you kissed Reid.

She couldn't deny that. Nor could she deny what had happened right after that, when the dream had drifted, and she had lost herself in the reality of Reid. Their lovemaking had erased everything else from her mind. Even now, she was thinking of Reid instead of finding the necklace. That had to stop.

As if he could sense her presence, Reid chose that moment to shift his gaze to the balcony of his room. When his gaze locked on hers, she felt her heart take a long tumble.

"Oh, my God," she whispered.

Alba rubbed her head against Nell's leg while she concentrated on drawing in a deep breath. When Reid turned his attention back to Daryl, she glanced at the dog. "It was only a dream. I didn't actually kiss him beneath the stones."

But in your heart you did. And in your heart...

Nell sank to her knees beside the dog. "I've fallen in love with him."

For a second, as the whispered words hung in the air, she felt her heart tumble again.

Maybe she'd never fallen out of love with him.

Following fast on that realization came a second. *Another day or two at the most—that's all you'll have.*

Pain sliced deeper this time. Alba licked her cheek. A few days. Beyond that, it was all blank pages.

Pages that you could write a different story on.

This time when she pressed a hand to her heart, it wasn't because of pain. It was because she was sure it had skipped a beat.

First things first.

She had to find that necklace. Rising, she shifted her gaze to the spot in the garden where the old gazebo had stood. Last night Daryl had made a salient point. If Eleanor had intended the portrait to be a treasure map to the location of the sapphires, she'd left the cave out. But there had to be some reason why Eleanor had chosen that spot to sit for her portrait. So it was still going to be the starting point of her search this morning.

Alba rubbed against her leg and whined. Glancing down, Nell saw that the dog had risen to her feet and had her eyes riveted on the terrace. Shifting her own gaze she watched Reid and Daryl rise from their chairs. A second later they were joined by her aunt Vi and a young man. A stranger.

"Good girl," she murmured as she patted the dog's head. "But you don't have to worry. He has to be the writer from the *Times*." As the young man sat down and crossed his legs, Nell felt a little flicker at the back of her mind. She'd experienced the same thing last night when she was looking at the time line Daryl had drawn. Narrowing her eyes, she studied the man more closely. He was several inches shorter than either Daryl or Reid and built along more slender lines. Nell agreed with Nurse Braxton—his face was indeed pretty, and the glasses added a geeky sexiness.

He was here to interview and shadow Vi, so then he could write a follow-up story on the discovery of Eleanor's earrings. And Nell was here to find the necklace and write The End on that story, she reminded herself. Her glance strayed back to Reid. The fastest route to filling in the blank pages on her subplot was to finish writing her main plot.

"The clock is ticking," she murmured to Alba. As she turned, her gaze ran over the writer from the *Times* again, and she remembered what it was that had been tugging at her mind. "The beginning," she said to the dog. "Every story has a trigger. I have to get dressed so I can talk to Reid." Then she dashed for the connecting door to her room.

REID KNEW THE instant that Nell disappeared from the window of his balcony. Not only had she vanished from his peripheral vision but he'd felt an immediate chill in the temperature of his skin when her gaze had left it.

Though Reid hadn't thought it possible, reading the fantasies she'd written on those pink sheets of paper had increased his desire for her. When he'd first caught sight of her on the balcony, he'd had to hold tight to the arms of his chair to keep himself from going to her.

Earlier when he had told Daryl his plans to take Nell to the gazebo, the older man had asked him to hang around long enough to get a personal impression of James Orbison. While Daryl had filled him in on the data the CIA had gathered on the young man, Vi had packed a canvas tote bag with a thermos of coffee and some of her scones so that he and Nell could head out to the gardens as soon as she woke up.

Ten minutes. That's what he'd give her to shower and dress. Ruthlessly he refocused his attention on the young journalist, and he found himself in agreement with Nurse Braxton's description—"pretty and preppy." The eyeglasses emphasized the intelligence in his eyes. Adding that to his unassuming air and enthusiasm about the castle, Reid understood why both Adair and Vi had been amenable to showing him the castle and the grounds, so he could write the initial story on their business and Eleanor's jewels.

What would Nell think of him?

Realizing that his thoughts had once more gone to

Nell, Reid prevented the frown from showing on his face. He hadn't been able to completely rid his mind of her, since he'd dug her mother's jewelry box out of the stones and unfolded those pink sheets of paper.

Entranced. Enchanted. Electrified. Those were just three of the words that described what he'd felt while he'd read them. She had an exceptional talent for creating images, and he'd recognized all of the settings—they were the places he and his brothers had played with the MacPherson sisters that long-ago summer. He'd never look at them the same way again. Especially not the gazebo. The memory of that tea party he'd attended when he was ten would be forever replaced by the scene she'd painted of undressing him slowly, inch by inch. Just thinking about it made his skin heat.

Instead of providing an answer to his questions, invading Nell's privacy had only complicated his problem. Now he burned with a desire to fulfill every one of her fantasies.

And more.

How in the hell had it come to this? Where had it all begun?

When Reid found himself tapping his fingers on the arm of his chair, he stilled them.

"You stopped by the hospital in Albany to see Deanna Lewis," Daryl was saying. "Why was that?"

Five more minutes, Reid decided. If Nell didn't appear, he'd make some excuse and go get her.

"Background information," Orbison said. "I like to be thorough in my research."

Reid thought of his mother's current project, and for the first time, his entire attention was captured by

James Orbison. "Have you had a chance to visit what's left of the Campbell estate in Scotland?"

"No. Much as I would like to go there, my editor couldn't approve that kind of expense. At least not yet. If I can parlay my articles into a book deal, that might change." He turned to Vi. "In the meantime, I'm perfectly happy to be doing research on *this* castle. I understand that your niece Nell is here visiting. I brought a copy of her book so she could sign it for me. I'd love to talk to her."

"I'm afraid that Nell won't be available. She's on a deadline." Reid leaned forward. "I can tell you what she'd ask if she were here. A writing question. What triggered your interest to write a story about the castle?"

"The Stuart sapphires, of course," Orbison replied with a smile.

"Where did you first hear about them?" Reid asked.

"I was a history major at Princeton, and I wrote my senior thesis on Mary Stuart. That's when I came across a photo of that painting that appeared in my article—the one of Mary Queen of Scots on her coronation day. When I saw Eleanor's portrait, I recognized the jewels immediately."

"Did you ever come across the means by which the sapphires came into the Campbells' possession?" Daryl asked.

Orbison shook his head. "No."

"What led you to Castle MacPherson?" Reid asked. "Before your article, the story of Eleanor's jewels has always been a local one."

Orbison's face brightened. "It was by pure chance. I was driving through the Adirondacks on an impromptu vacation, and I stopped at the diner in Glen Loch. They were talking about the new wedding destination business that was being launched at the castle. By the time we finished our pancakes, I'd heard all about the legend and the story of how Angus built the castle for Eleanor. The owner of the diner, Edie, even had a copy of Nell's book. When someone mentioned the sapphires' connection to Mary Stuart, I called my editor and pitched him the idea of writing a feature article on the castle. He went for it."

The explanation was plausible enough. Reid knew Daryl by now, and he would check every detail.

And where was Nell? More than ten minutes had passed. Had she gone out to the gazebo on her own? Panic had him rising from the table abruptly. "Excuse me," he murmured as he strode toward the sliding glass doors to the kitchen. "There's a call I have to make."

On his way through the kitchen, Reid grabbed the thermos of coffee Vi had made and then increased his pace as he entered the hallway to the central foyer. He was three strides past the open door to the main parlor before he fully registered that Nell was standing in front of Eleanor's portrait.

Stopping, he made himself draw in a deep breath. A cool head was essential if he was going to be able to do his job. When he stepped into the room, she didn't move. Neither did Alba, who was lying at her feet. "I thought you'd gone ahead without me," he finally said.

"No." Nell didn't turn to face him. She was too busy analyzing why it hadn't even occurred to her to go out there to the gazebo by herself. A few days ago, the story would have been different. She would have snatched the opportunity to prove that she could find the necklace on her own. Now Reid's opinion and his ideas were important to her. She'd even grown impatient while she'd been waiting for him to join her.

"I stopped here to gather my thoughts before joining you on the terrace." Clasping her hands together, she finally met his eyes. "But if I *had* left you behind, it would have been tit for tat. You left me to meet with that journalist."

"I was doing my job." He opened the thermos and poured coffee for her while he filled her in on their successful search for the bullet. "What thoughts are you gathering? Have you changed your mind about the gazebo?"

"No. I still have a feeling that it plays an important part in the message that Eleanor left. It has to be a part of the puzzle. Otherwise, why choose that place to sit for her portrait? But seeing that journalist made me think about Daryl's time line and where everything to do with Eleanor's sapphires started." She pointed at the whiteboard. "We've been concentrating on Adair's discovery of the first earring and the *Times* article that made everything public. Those two events triggered all that's happened here at the castle. But my thought is the real beginning has to go back to when Eleanor first wore those jewels. We know that she had them with her on the night she and Angus eloped. But we still don't know how the Campbell family came to possess them."

Reid turned to study the portrait. "Right. Cam called last night and told me there's a portrait gallery of all the Campbell heirs and their families, including one of Eleanor's parents and her sisters. The sapphires don't appear in any of the paintings."

"What if they had never belonged to the Campbells? If they had, surely the family would have wanted it known. Mary Stuart wore them in a painting celebrating her coronation. Eleanor wore them in this portrait. And she was wearing them in the dream I had last night."

"What kind of dream?"

"She was dancing in a massive ballroom with a man. Not the ballroom here. There was a huge fire burning in a fireplace and candles everywhere. I'd swear that the dress she was wearing is the one she's wearing in the painting. He looked familiar, but it definitely wasn't Angus. Then the ballroom faded. Eleanor was kissing Angus beneath the stone arch, and she was wearing the same dress and the sapphires."

When Reid said nothing, Nell shot him a sideways look. "I know dreams aren't evidence. I know their meaning is at best symbolic. But look at the evidence we do have.

"No one is wearing them in the portrait gallery. Your mother hasn't found any mention of them in the records that remain in the library. And she hasn't come across any stories about them that have been handed down orally. Jewels like those sapphires generate talk. The legend of the stone arch is still being told—there and here. But the only place where there are stories about the Stuart sapphires is here."

"Mom isn't having any luck discovering the story behind Angus and Eleanor's flight, either." He poured her a refill out of the thermos. "Deanna Lewis claimed they were never Eleanor's dowry. What do you think happened?"

After taking a sip of coffee, she said, "Maybe they were a gift from this strange man she was dancing with in my dream. I might write it that way. It would certainly complicate everything."

"It would explain why the jewels didn't appear in any of the Campbell portraits," Reid said.

"But it doesn't explain the lack of stories. Whoever they belonged to must have been furious when they disappeared. Murders have occurred for less. Wars have started for less. Someone must have gone to a great deal of trouble to keep that story hushed up."

"Someone may still be trying to keep it a secret. That may be why there was a fire in the library on the Campbell estate six months ago," Reid mused. "It might also be a reason why someone spent so much time searching through the library here at the castle. Eleanor and Angus had to have known the story behind the sapphires. If she kept a journal…"

Nell grabbed his hand. "That's what they might have been looking for. If this Gwendolen 'Campbell' really is a true descendent of the Campbell line, she wouldn't want anyone to know who might have a better claim on those sapphires."

"It still doesn't explain why she thinks she has a better claim than you and your sisters," Reid pointed out.

"Once we find the necklace, and she makes a play for it, we can ask her. Let's go."

The moment Nell opened the front door, Alba nosed her way through it, then turned and waited for them to follow.

Nell sighed. "Like it or not, it looks like I've picked up another guardian angel."

Reid laughed as they headed toward the gardens.

13

THE MOMENT HE pushed aside the branches of the hedge so that Nell could slip through them, Reid's senses went on full alert. Even as he tightened his grip on her hand, he noticed the disturbed dirt in the spot where he'd unearthed the flat stone step. "Someone has been here since I left."

Nell sent Reid an amused glance. "I would imagine so. I can't recall the last time I visited this place."

"I was here about an hour ago to check out security." Keeping her close to his side, he circled to the spot and pointed at it. "I pushed enough debris away to uncover what must have been one of the steps that led up to the wooden floor. Someone has shoved it all back in place."

"You were here alone?" She poked a finger into his chest. "Who checked out the security for you?"

When she poked him again, he captured her hand. "I had to look at the place, make a plan to keep you safe." He swept his gaze along the top of the hedge to the hills beyond. "The sun was barely up. Skinner's men would have still been looking for the casings in the area above the stone arch. Whoever it was used the shadows and the trees for cover." He cursed himself silently that none of that had entered his mind while he'd been checking out the security. He'd been too distracted by the idea of reading Nell's fantasies.

Nell slipped her hand into his and held it tight. "He was probably watching you from the time you left the castle this morning. When you came here alone, he could have killed you."

"Or vice versa. I wouldn't have made such an easy target this morning. And while Skinner's men might not have spotted him, they were up there in the hills. Any kind of noise would have brought them down."

Nell swept her gaze along the tops of the hedges. "I'm betting he never left the area. After he shot at you last night, he could have slipped down into the garden and just waited."

She was right. There were plenty of places to take cover in the garden. In his mind, Reid planned the conversation he'd have with Skinner and Daryl. Some of the volunteers would have to patrol the paths, especially during the wedding rehearsal.

"I want to get you back to the castle, but we have to look for the necklace," Nell said.

Reid looked at her. "You want to get *me* back to the castle? Who's the bodyguard here?"

"We both are. But you're the one who got shot at. Whoever he is, he's smart. But he's not here now. We can relax for the moment."

"Why do you say that?"

"If he were still here in the garden, Alba would be raising the alarm." She patted the dog's head. "Vi claims her instincts are spot-on."

Reid glanced around. The sun was higher in the sky.

Even in camouflage, an intruder was likely to be spotted by the volunteers patrolling the hills. Alba was walking around the perimeter of the stones that had formed the base of the old gazebo, sniffing as she went. Every so often, she paused to dig in the dirt, but she showed no signs of alarm.

"Let's just make it fast," he said. "I was thinking about Daryl's point that the cliff face isn't in the painting, and I want to show you something." He led her to the far side of the circle formed by the stones. "Turn around." Once she had, he gripped her waist and lifted her up so she sat on his shoulder.

"I'm thinking this is about the height of the bench Eleanor sat on for her portrait. The stone arch is beyond her right shoulder. Tell me what you see."

"The castle, the woods and the cliffs beyond. To the right, I can see the arch, more hills above it, to the left, the lake. She could see pretty much everything from here."

"Think of the position of her head in the painting. What is she directly facing?" Reid prompted.

Nell shaded her eyes. "The top of the cliff where the cave is. It's directly beyond the third floor of castle. She must have been looking straight at it." The thrill in her tone gave Reid a great deal of satisfaction. He lowered her then. Her feet had barely touched the ground when Alba began to bark excitedly.

Reid shoved her behind him, pulled out his gun and fanned it in a quick circle. Then he pushed Nell down behind the biggest pile of stones and checked the garden paths on each side of the tall hedges. No sign of anyone. Only the continued barking of the dog marred the silence.

Turning back, he saw Alba pawing the dirt near the stone step he'd uncovered on his earlier visit.

"She's found something." Dropping to her knees, Nell pushed more dirt aside. Sunlight glinted off metal as she lifted Alba's unearthed treasure in the palm of her hand.

"Another earring. And it's not Eleanor's." She met Reid's eyes. "My autograph lady was wearing this when she asked me to sign that book."

Alba barked as she pawed at the dirt again. Sunlight glinted off metal again as Reid squatted down beside Nell. But it wasn't jewelry he saw in the little depression. It was a very sophisticated electronic listening device.

"What—?"

Reid silenced Nell by putting a hand over her mouth. Keeping her eyes on his, she wrapped her fingers around his wrist and tightened them. *Good girl,* he thought. He mouthed the words, "Follow my lead."

Something flashed into her eyes. Not fear, but excitement.

He wanted to kiss her. *Later,* he promised himself.

Someone had listened to everything they'd said. In his mind, he quickly reviewed the essentials of their conversation and wished he had more time to strategize. "Well, now our villain has a face. That will make it easier for Sheriff Skinner's men if she tries to get on the grounds again."

That would give her something to worry about. She would know now that they'd put it together that she had to have been involved in the attempted hit-and-run on Piper.

"We just need to find out who she is." He wanted

their listener worried but not in panic mode. "How sure are you that the necklace has to be here in the foundation of the gazebo?" he asked Nell.

Reid saw the surprise flash into Nell's eyes, then something else. Understanding? Amusement? She didn't miss a beat before saying, "I'm absolutely positive. I think Eleanor planned where she would hide the jewels right from this very spot. It's just a matter of finding the necklace before someone else in my family is hurt."

"C'mon," he said. "Let's go fill your aunt in on our discoveries."

AN HOUR LATER, Nell sat on the couch in the main parlor trying to make her mind go blank. It was a technique she sometimes used when she had to write a scene and too many possibilities were flooding her mind. Daryl and Reid had been discussing them nonstop since Reid had hurried her back to the castle. As a precautionary measure, the two men had searched the room thoroughly for any listening devices, and now they were on their cell phones. Daryl had his pressed to his ear while he stood sentry at the French doors that connected the parlor with Adair's office. Through the sheer curtains on the panes of glass, he could keep an unobtrusive eye on Vi and James Orbison as her aunt dealt with a young couple interested in scheduling their wedding at the castle.

At least that meeting seemed to be going well. She only wished her meeting with Daryl and Reid had gone as well. But from the moment Reid had rushed her away from the gazebo and back to the castle, he and Daryl had done all the talking and decision-making. The only time they'd paid her any heed was when she'd advanced the possibility that autograph lady had been the shooter.

Two full beats of silence followed her suggestion. She'd almost heard the wheels turning in their heads as she'd made her case. "The dropped earring makes us assume she lost it when she was planting the listening device. Why didn't she assign that task to her 'accomplice' with the military training? Unless there was no accomplice?"

At that point both men had gone to their cell phones. Neither had spoken to her since. She was beginning to feel like Jane Eyre standing out in the cold and peering through the windows at the life she would never be a part of.

Her gaze settled on the gold earring on the coffee table, and once again she experienced the same icy sliver of fear she'd felt when she had first recognized it. It was her desire to keep her family safe that had kept her from getting angry that the two men were excluding her.

But she had spent the past year establishing an independent life for herself and wasn't going to let anyone make all the decisions for her again. She would have to show them that her ideas were just as good as theirs. Maybe better.

"The landscaper will begin excavating the foundation within the hour," Reid said as he pocketed his cell phone and joined Daryl at the French doors. "That should buy us some time."

Nothing to argue with there, Nell thought.

Daryl removed his cell phone from his ear. "Skinner's men will have pictures of Gwendolen within the hour. My man is still researching, but her most recent husband had a brother who served in the British army. U.K. special forces. But the brother-in-law died six months ago."

Enough, Nell thought. Once again, they were talking as if she weren't in the room. Rising, she said, "He could have taught her to shoot, supplied her with a weapon and night vision goggles at the very least. And six months seems to be a magic number in all of this."

When both men turned to look at her, it gave Nell a great deal of satisfaction. While she had their attention, she moved quickly to the original time line that Daryl had drawn on the whiteboard. "The article in the *Times* that triggered all the interest in the Stuart sapphires appeared about six months ago. The fire in the library on the Campbell estate in Scotland occurred six months ago. And now we find out our lead suspect's brother-in-law with a military background died at roughly the same time. Coincidence? I sure couldn't sell it that way in a book."

"You think our Gwendolen was behind that fire?" Daryl asked.

Reid turned to Daryl. "I share Nell's aversion to coincidence. Her theory is that someone discovered something about the location and the story behind how the sapphires came into Eleanor's possession in the library at the Campbell estate, and then set a fire to suppress the details. Before that they may have discovered a clue that pointed toward where the jewels are."

"And they believed that the library here might also contain some of the details," Daryl said. "Or hold the key to the location of the jewels—until they started popping up elsewhere."

"So far I'm just thinking about possible story scenarios," Nell said. "But if Gwendolen is the master-mind behind everything, as a successful grifter, she's become very adept at using what comes to hand—circumstances, people. I'll bet Duncan would agree."

"I'll update him on what we're thinking." Reid punched a number into his phone. Then he turned to Nell. "In the meantime, fill us in on what you're thinking."

The type of warmth that flooded her at Reid's words was new. "As a con woman, she's played a lot of different roles, probably picked up many skills along the way. The image she presents to the public—the fashionably dressed matron—is only one of her personas." Nell leaned over and picked up the gold earring, holding it so that it caught the light. "My first impression was that she would make a great villain because she looks so *normal*. A matron who dresses well, who wants a book signed for her granddaughter, who does volunteer work at hospitals. But she also has a string of dead ex-husbands. Not to mention a deceased brother-in-law."

There was a beat of silence as the two men exchanged a glance.

"Nell is very good at spinning stories," Reid said. "I don't like this one, but it fits the facts."

"There's another thing," Nell said. "The person who visited the castle library over a period of six months was patient. She's not patient anymore. She sent her step-daughter in to kidnap Piper. She had another accomplice try to run Piper down. Now she's doing things herself."

Reid looked at Daryl. "I don't know why we need Duncan when we've got a behavioral analyst right in the room."

She was back in the game, Nell thought. Now, if she could just convince them to let her go to the gazebo…

"I'll put another man on it. I want to know how those husbands died, and what kind of skill sets she might have picked up from them." Daryl was punching a number into his cell when Alba rose to her feet and whined. He glanced through the French doors, then at his watch. "Vi is through with her clients, and the wedding party should be arriving at any minute for the rehearsal. She'll want to greet them. I'll go with her and Orbison. I want the two of you to stay here." He shifted his gaze from Reid to Nell and then back again. "Consider yourselves under house arrest."

"But the sapphires aren't in the house," Nell said. "And I'm supposed to find them. Reid?"

"I agree with Daryl. More than twenty-four hours have passed. Once we start excavating the old gazebo, Gwendolen may decide we know where the necklace is, and we're finding it. Or she may believe we've already found it and we're stalling. Either way, she's going to have to make a move soon. Planting that listening device was very risky. And you're dead-on about her waning patience. If she still believes you're the key to the necklace, she'll make a move on you."

The words chilled Nell to the bone. Reid was right. She couldn't have written it any better. But how was she supposed to find Eleanor's necklace if they kept her locked up in the castle?

"The castle's security is state-of-the-art," Daryl said. "She's not getting in here. Skinner will have men posted at every entrance during the wedding rehearsal. And that will take place at the stone arch. All you have to do is stay put."

When Daryl exited through the French doors, Alba gave a whine, but she stayed right where she was.

"Looks like the dog agrees that we're the ones in danger," Nell said.

"Her instincts are good. And you can save whatever arguments you're summoning up. I'm not going to take you to the gazebo." He began to pace. "If your theory is right, she's not just a class A con woman with some idea that those sapphires belong to her. She's a stone-cold killer. When she tried to have Piper killed yesterday, it wasn't just because you didn't get up here to the castle fast enough. I'm betting it was because Piper was responsible for putting her stepdaughter in a coma. It was a pretty good plan. Motivate you and get revenge at the same time."

Nell thought she couldn't feel any colder, but his words about her sister made her tremble. "I didn't even think of that. You're scaring me."

"Good." Reid moved to her, then pulled her into his arms and held on tight. It was something he'd wanted to do ever since he'd gotten her back safely into the castle. "I'm scaring myself."

"Piper—"

"She'll be safe. Gwendolen is here focused on the necklace." Which meant that Nell was the one in danger.

When she wrapped her arms around him and held him as tightly as he was holding her, he couldn't have named all the feelings rushing through him. Not the passion that he'd felt, not the explosion of desire that she could so easily trigger. This was what he'd felt when he'd awakened with her in his arms—that warmth moving through his veins with the slow but powerful strength of a river that couldn't be held back or denied.

He wanted this; perhaps he'd wanted it from the first moment he saw her.

He would want this always.

Drawing back, he met her gaze. What he hoped he saw was that she was experiencing the same thing he was.

He wanted to ask her. But the timing was wrong. Her life was in danger. He knew that. But he also knew that it wasn't just fear for her safety that was holding him back. It was his fear of her answer. It was that and that alone that made him release her for the moment and step back.

"We need to find the necklace." He put his hands on her shoulders to turn her to face the portrait. "You believe she put the clues in the portrait. So let's go back to square one. What story is Eleanor telling in the painting?"

Nell had to shove down the urge to object. He was correct. But if he hadn't drawn back, if he hadn't turned her to face the painting, the desire to stay in his arms would have kept her there. She might have given anything to stay right there. She might have given *everything*.

That realization helped her focus. Everything wasn't what he wanted. It wasn't what she believed she wanted, either.

"Tell me Eleanor's story," Reid prompted.

Pushing everything else from her mind, she tried to imagine she was seeing Eleanor's portrait for the first time.

"Talk me through it as if you were writing about it."

"I see a beautiful woman. My eye is drawn immediately to her. And then to the sapphires."

"What do you notice next?"

"Her hair, the dress. It's white like a wedding dress. She wants to remind us of her story. The stone arch in the background—that's her history, and it's the symbol of the love that triggered everything."

"Go on."

"The expression on her face. She's glowing. So are the sapphires. She wants us to know how happy she is, and she wants to tell us about the sapphires. A picture limits the scope of the story she can tell. That makes the details even more significant."

"What else?"

"Her— How slender she is, how small her hands are, the way her fingers curl over that pile of books." Nell felt her hands tense. "I'm starting to babble."

Reid squeezed her shoulders. "Relax. Don't think or edit. Just list the details."

"The flowers. She's sitting in the gazebo in a garden that she designed and planted. She's looking right at the cliff where the cave is. The third floor of the castle is also in her line of vision. But…"

"What?"

"The stone arch is in her past. I'm not surprised that she hid one of the earrings there because it's the connection between where she and Angus fell in love and the life they built here. But her present and her future—that's what she's looking at. It's almost like another painting. The castle is in the foreground and the cliff beyond. The cave must have meant something to them. Perhaps it was a place where she and Angus could sneak off to."

"Keep going."

Nell closed her eyes and reimagined the view she'd

had in those moments when she'd sat on Reid's shoulders at the gazebo. "She can see the glint of water at the top of Tinker's Falls. The lake. The hills surrounding the castle—they're all there either in her line of vision or in the painting." Her stomach sank. She opened her eyes to focus on Reid. "Thinking of it that way, she's got everything in there but the kitchen sink. How in the world are we supposed to figure out where she hid the necklace?"

"Look again."

She stared at the portrait once more. Her gaze focused automatically on Eleanor first. "Odd. She's so relaxed but her hands are tense on those books." Nell felt her own fingers curl and grow tense again. "She's the focus of the portrait, and other than the sapphires, they're the closest thing to her. Why are they even there?"

"The illustrations in your book—could those be the books you found them in?" Reid asked.

"They could be. They're in my mother's room." The image flashed into her mind of exactly what she'd seen when she'd been sitting on Reid's shoulders in the gazebo. And she could have sworn that the glow on Eleanor's face grew even brighter. Excitement bloomed inside Nell as she grabbed Reid's hand and pulled him into the foyer. "She wasn't just looking at the cliff face. She was looking right at that room."

14

REID HAD TO hurry his pace to keep up with her. To his surprise she didn't stop on the second floor where her own room was and instead climbed a third flight of stairs. At the top was a double set of doors carved in oak. Opening them, she brushed aside cobwebs, then led the way down a dim hallway.

"When my mother was alive, the nursery was on this floor and so was the master suite my parents used. When she died, my father declared the whole third floor of the castle off-limits. He locked up the library, too, because it had been her favorite room."

The room she ushered Reid into was dim. Sunlight struggled with grime on the windows and barely illuminated the dust motes in its path. He took in the perfectly made bed, the robe that still lay across its foot. His heart twisted when he made out the tiny white crib tucked into a book-lined alcove in one wall.

"As far as I know, I'm the only one who's visited this place since my mother died."

"Your sisters never came up here?" A rumble of thunder had him striding to the windows that ran along two walls. Alba followed, her collar jingling. "It's just a storm, girl," he murmured as he patted her head. He knew that she couldn't hear the thunder or his words but could feel the rumble effects. Still she jumped up and settled herself on the window seats that lined one wall of windows. On the other, sliding glass doors opened onto a balcony with a stunning view of the lake. From this height, he could clearly make out the hedge circling the old gazebo. Beyond that, a small group of people had gathered around Vi and Daryl in front of the stone arch. The wedding rehearsal was about to begin. Thunder rumbled again. He patted the dog's head. There wasn't a cloud in the sky.

"Adair and Piper said coming up here would make them too sad."

Turning, he watched her run her hand along the railing of the tiny white crib. "How old were you when she died?" he asked.

"Six months. I don't remember her at all. I must have been four or five when I realized Piper and Adair did, and I couldn't. It made me feel left out, so that's when I started sneaking up here. I suppose I was hoping something might trigger a memory. I even tried playing dress up in her clothes. Nothing worked."

"But you kept coming back anyway."

She smiled as she joined him at the windows. "It was forbidden. That held a great deal of appeal. And I found other things I liked to do. Like reading. My mother's favorite room was the library, and I pretended the books on those shelves in the alcove were her favorites. I read them all. On rainy days, I used to sit on this window seat and write. Eleanor did some of her sketches right from this vantage point."

"The sketchbooks. You found them in the alcove?"

"No. I found them in what I've always imagined was her secret cupboard. You've seen Angus's secret cupboard in the main parlor."

Nell moved to the stone fireplace that took up a great deal of the wall opposite the alcove. "It's different than Angus's. It's built right into the side of the fireplace."

Angus's secret cupboard had fascinated Reid's brothers and him when they were ten. Only it wasn't a secret. According to Cam, Piper had made a show-and-tell video when she was in fifth grade that was available in the local library.

By the time he joined Nell, she had swung open one of the square flat stones on a central hinge just large enough to allow her to slide the sketchbooks out. Dropping to his knees, he ran his hand along the inside of the space. His best guess was that it was about two feet square. Smaller than Angus's. Smooth stones lined the walls, and not one of them budged.

"If Eleanor's necklace were in there, I would have found it when I discovered the sketchbooks." Nell carried them to the window seat.

"Just checking. Why don't we split these up?" As he sat beside her, there was an ominous roll of thunder. Alba inched close enough to make contact with his thigh. Sunlight still poured down on the gardens, but he could see a line of black clouds on the far side of the lake rolling forward like invading tanks. A car pulled into the drive and a young woman stepped out, followed by two older women. Reid recognized one of them as Edie. He noted that Daryl was talking with Sheriff Skinner. Thunder growled again and wind gusts disturbed the leaves in the garden.

"I hope that storm doesn't interfere with the rehearsal," Nell said as she passed him a book.

Reid began to turn the pages. Some of the drawings he recognized from Nell's book. Other places captured in the sketches he remembered seeing the summer he was ten. "I'm noticing a pattern. Many of them are drawn from the vantage point of the gazebo. But Eleanor must have done others right on the scene. It's almost as if she was using the drawings the way a photographer might use a camera—taking the wide angle shot and then zooming in.

"You're right." Nell pointed to the page she was studying. "Here's the one of the castle and the cliffs. Then on the next page there's one of the beach that had to have been drawn from that ledge in front of the cave. Then there are several of the interior sections of the cave. I'll bet one of them was where Piper and Duncan discovered the earring. It's almost as though she's drawing a treasure map right to that earring with her sketches."

Reid turned to look at her, once again all admiration at the quick way her mind worked. "Did you ever tell anyone about these drawings or show them to anyone?"

"No. When I was trying to convince my editor and publishers to use the drawings, I showed them enlarged photos. I never told anyone about the secret cupboard, either."

"Not even your sisters?"

"Especially not my sisters. I told my publisher and the marketing people that I'd found them in the library. Sometimes I felt guilty about not telling Piper and Adair. But by the time I had found them, I'd begun to think of this place as mine—a secret I shared only with my mother and Eleanor. Don't you have secrets you've kept from your brothers?"

He smiled. "I treasure each and every one of them." Setting aside the book, he rose and walked over to the fireplace. Kneeling down, he pushed the stone back into place. The mechanism worked smoothly. Even when he ran his hands over it, he felt nothing that indicated that there was a secret cupboard behind it.

"It's constructed very well. Assuming that Eleanor hid the sketchbooks here, I still wonder why no one ever found them or why this secret cupboard didn't become part of the family history the way Angus's did. How did you discover the way to work that stone?"

"Totally by accident. There was a huge rainstorm that day just like the one that seems to be blowing in now. We lost electricity for a few minutes. During one flash of lightning, I noticed a glint along this side of the fireplace. When the lights came back on, I investigated. The stone swung open quite easily, and there they were."

Thunder clapped overhead, and wind howled its way past the windows. Alba pressed closer to her. For a while Nell watched Reid try to find the way to open the stone and was surprised that he couldn't.

"I'll show you." Nell joined him and slipped just the tips of her fingers between two of the stones. The stone swung open again.

"Let me try." Once he closed the stone, he did try, but the size of his fingers prevented him from getting any traction. "It seems to require a woman's touch," he murmured.

The ringing of his cell was nearly drowned out by another clap of thunder overhead.

Reid held the phone so Nell could hear. "Change of

plans," Daryl said. "Vi's bringing the wedding rehearsal inside to the ballroom. Skinner will make sure the rest of the castle is blocked off, but his job will be easier if you and Nell join us. That way we can all multitask."

"Agreed." He ended the call and the instant he studied Nell's eyes, he saw mirrored in them exactly what he was feeling—disappointment and frustration.

"I need to keep looking through the sketches. The answer is in them somewhere."

"I think so, too." There wasn't a doubt in his mind that Eleanor was somehow going to guide Nell to the necklace. "We'll come back just as soon as we can. And we'll come back together, Nell. Promise?"

"Promise. Let me put the sketchbooks back."

Once she did, he signaled the dog, and they left the room.

"YOUR AUNT VI's a genius," Sheriff Skinner said.

"Yes." Nell had always known that, but the quick way Vi had improvised to go forward with the wedding rehearsal in the ballroom confirmed it in spades. Nell could only hope that the rest of the rehearsal would go as swiftly. She needed to get back to those sketchbooks.

There were twenty or so people in the ballroom. They'd all pitched in to line up folding chairs into a makeshift aisle. Now they were standing in small groups laughing and chatting—totally ignoring the storm that raged outside. Daryl had shut Alba away in the kitchen because she'd started growling and barking when the wedding party had descended on the castle.

At the far end of the room, Vi stood in a huddle with the bride and groom and the minister. Nearby, Nell spotted Edie with a concerned look on her face as she gave

James Orbison a pat on his arm. The young journalist was maximizing on the chaos produced by the sudden change of venue to speak to as many guests as he could.

Reid and Daryl stood nearby the line of French doors that opened onto a long terrace with a view of the lake. Rain pounded against the windowpanes, and lightning crisscrossed the sky. A pretty young flute player began to play softly—Beethoven's "Ode to Joy" as Edie and the groom's father, Benjy Grimshaw, joined Reid and Daryl. From this distance, Nell could see that Edie was making the introductions. The conversation was brief, but when the couple walked away, both Daryl and Reid reached immediately for their cell phones.

Turning to Sheriff Skinner, Nell asked, "Do you know what Benjy Grimshaw discovered about the gun the shooter used?"

"One of his blog followers in England is all but positive that the bullets were manufactured there," Skinner said. "He claims he has a rifle in his pawn shop that uses that particular caliber. The weapon is a favorite with upper-class Brits who love to hunt."

"Gwendolen could have access to that kind of bullet. She might even own that kind of gun. But it's not proof."

"No," Skinner agreed. "But the evidence is piling up."

Not fast enough, Nell thought. Thunder continued to rumble as Reid and Daryl talked into their cells, gathering that needed evidence. Frustration that she had thought she'd quelled rose up again. Not because Daryl and Reid were leaving her out. Their splitting off made perfect sense. As long as there was an unplanned event going on in the castle, they had to focus on security. For everyone.

The source of her frustration was more personal. Oh, she wanted to tell herself that it was because she was so close to finding the necklace, and she wanted Reid's perspective on the sketches. He would see things that she couldn't. The last thing she'd expected was that they made a good team. They were so different. But somehow they fit. Perfectly.

He stood not fifty feet away from her, and yet she missed him.

How in the world had it come to that? What had become of her goal to operate independently? How had she gotten to the point where she wanted to be with him all the time? She hated to think of herself as that… immersed.

She studied his frame in the window, the darkness of the storm at his back. The toughness and the strength in his face and his body offered such an appealing contrast to the kindness she'd always known was there. A kaleidoscope of images flashed through her mind. His face as it had looked on the day their parents had married and again when she'd first seen him talking to the policeman at the door of Piper's apartment. The expression in his eyes when he'd walked through the door to her room last night, and finally what she'd seen in his eyes after he'd held her in the main parlor only hours ago.

Her heart took a long bounce. There was a story in the way he looked at her, but she'd avoided thinking about it. Afraid that she might be seeing in his eyes what she wanted to see—the narrative of her own developing feelings and not his. Images always told stories, but love was blind. Her heart bounced again, and fear bubbled up.

The slow crescendo in the sound of a flute had the

guests quieting, and Nell's attention switched to Vi as she led the bride, her father and two other young women to the end of the makeshift aisle. The groom-to-be and another man stood to the left of the minister. While the music played softly, Vi orchestrated the seating of the groom's parents and then the bride's. Two young men were quietly capturing each moment on their cell phones.

Something flickered at the edge of her mind, then faded before she could grasp it.

Focus, she told herself. Find the necklace, and then you'll figure out what to do about Reid Sutherland.

REID PUNCHED HIS contact button for Cam. Calculating the time difference, he figured that his brother and Adair were meeting with the housekeeper's mother right now, and depending on where the woman lived, cell reception could be tricky.

A few minutes ago, he and Daryl had discovered they'd been told a lie. Not a major one, but it was enough to put his senses on full alert. Daryl was checking it out. But Reid had an urgent question for his brother. His gaze swept the room. As the flute player segued into the wedding march, Vi gently urged the first bridesmaid up the aisle.

"Problem or favor?" Cam asked in his ear.

"Both. What have you found out about the sapphires?"

"A word to the wise—housekeepers and servants know everything. Delia Dunsmore is ninety-four years old, but her mind still works like a steel trap. Mom's in love with her, and A.D. wants to paint her."

Reid suppressed the urge to tell his brother to hurry

up. He knew from experience doing that would only have the opposite effect. Instead, he checked the room once again. Everyone was accounted for. Security was tight. Skinner was still at Nell's side. Reminding himself of those things only increased the urgency he felt in his gut. Time was running out.

"Is that the wedding march I hear in the background? You're not getting hitched to Nell, are you?" Cam asked.

Ignoring the question, Reid took a risk. "Could you give me the *Reader's Digest* version? Was this Delia able to recall anything about how the Campbells gained possession of the sapphires?"

"They were a betrothal gift from Eleanor's groom-to-be, one Alistair MacGregor. He'd been invited to the castle and had fallen in love with Eleanor on sight. On the night of the ball celebrating their engagement, he gave them to her and insisted she wear them. Evidently, his family had been staunch supporters of the queen, and the sapphires had been a gift to his great-great-grandfather from Mary Stuart herself. According to Delia, the marriage would have brought money and land to help the Campbells over a rough patch."

Reid recalled Nell's dream. "So she was wearing them on the night of the big betrothal ball, and that was the same night she ran off with Angus."

"Correct. Technically, it could be argued that she had a right to take the jewels with her."

"I wonder if Eleanor would make that argument. Or her betrothed. If those sapphires were mine, and the woman I loved ran off with them and another man, I wouldn't take that generous a view. Why wasn't more of a stink raised?"

"Alistair MacGregor hanged himself. One of the servants discovered him on the morning after the party. According to Delia it was all hushed up. Guests at the betrothal bash were told that the bride and groom had decided to elope and move immediately to his isolated estate in northern Scotland. Since Alistair was an only child and the last of his line, no one from that side offered a different version. Scandal avoided. Delia says that for months the Campbell family waited for Eleanor to return. If she had, they probably would have hidden her away in a nunnery and kept the jewels."

"Who inherited on the MacGregor side?" Reid asked. "Seems to me that part of the family might think they have a claim, especially if there's no written record to support the story that the sapphires were a gift to Eleanor."

"We're all going to work on that. But if there was a written record, that might have been what Castle MacPherson's nocturnal visitor was looking for in the library."

"And it may be the reason why a fire came close to destroying the library at the Campbell estate," Reid pointed out. "That's why I called. I need to know if anyone visited the Campbell estate six to eight months ago. Nell and I both think that the fire in the library is related to what's going on now."

"Hold on," Cam said. "I can ask the housekeeper right now."

While he waited, Reid glanced around the ballroom again. The second bridesmaid was halfway up the aisle. Sheriff Skinner still stood at Nell's side. Everyone else was focused on the progress of the rehearsal. Nothing he saw triggered an alarm. Still, a sense of urgency rolled through him, and he willed Cam to hurry.

His gaze settled on Nell. More than anything he wanted to go to her and just carry her away. But he couldn't. Gut instinct told him that she was very close to figuring out where that necklace was. He was as sure of that as he was that something unforeseen was about to happen.

"How are you holding up?" Skinner asked.

Nell dragged her gaze away from the two young people at the altar to look at Sheriff Skinner. "I just wish this was over. I need to find that necklace."

"If anyone can figure out where it is, you can," Skinner commented.

Surprised, she met his eyes. "You sound so sure of that."

"You're a lot like your mother."

"You knew her?" Even as she asked it, she realized it was a foolish question. She judged Sheriff Skinner to be close to her father's age, and everyone knew everyone in Glen Loch.

"I dated her a few times in high school before your father snapped her up."

Something in his tone made her ask, "Were you in love with her?"

"Enough to start thinking I should seal the deal by kissing her up here under the stones. She was sixteen, I was seventeen, and I thought I had time."

"What happened?"

There was a twinkle in Skinner's eyes. "Your father had some fast moves, and he had the home-court advantage."

She'd never thought of her father in that way, as a young man in love. And she'd certainly never thought of him as having fast moves. "Maybe it was my mother who had the fast moves."

Skinner chuckled. "You could be right. Once she set a goal for herself, she never let anyone stop her."

When the flute player segued into the bridal march, Nell shifted her gaze back to the wedding rehearsal just in time to see the bride-to-be and her father start up the aisle.

"Molly's two younger brothers are getting everything on their cell phones," Sheriff Skinner commented. "With that newfangled technology and zoom feature, those little phones can do videos and stills, and they don't have to run around the way wedding photographers had to do in my day."

A zoom feature. Now Nell knew exactly what she'd been trying to remember just before the sheriff had joined her. She and Reid had already theorized that was exactly what Eleanor had done. The location of the necklace had to be in that final sketchbook. If she couldn't get to the sketches, she'd just summon them up in her mind. Closing her eyes, she focused on the drawings in the last book.

The location of the necklace would be in one of the close-ups. Not in the gazebo. She couldn't recall even one sketch that Eleanor had made of it. But from that perspective she'd sketched the castle several times. Then Nell remembered one series of drawings and a close-up, one that she hadn't used in her book because she had never wanted to share it.

The necklace would be there. She was sure of it.

A spattering of applause broke out as the bride-to-be's father handed her over to the groom-to-be. Then glass shattered and screams mingled with the sound of glass shattering again.

"Get down," Skinner shouted. "Everybody, get down."

Nell had no choice when the sheriff shoved her to the floor. "Stay here," he said as he crouched low and moved away. Keeping her head on the floor, Nell searched for a glimpse of Reid. Too many chairs stood in the way. Lightning flashed as another pane of glass splintered into shards. Fear froze Nell's stomach as she saw the silhouetted figure and the rifle poised on the far end of the terrace just where the land dropped away to the lake below. Another pane of glass on the French doors shattered very close to where Reid had been standing.

A hand clamped on her wrist and a voice rasped in her ear. "My partner's next bullet will hit Reid if you don't come with me now."

AT THE SOUND of the first shot, Reid pitched to the floor, and rolled twice until he could use a potted plant for some cover. Then he pulled his gun. He couldn't see anyone outside the French doors, but the sniper could be crouching behind the stone wall that ran the length of the terrace. The lights inside the ballroom made them all sitting targets. A quick glance over his shoulder assured him that Nell was out of sight.

There were woods to the right of the terrace. In his mind, he could see just how the shooter had taken advantage of the storm and gotten in position. Wait for everyone to be on the move, take out the volunteer Skinner had stationed at the back of the castle and then wait for the moment to shoot.

Nell. A mix of panic and fear sprinted up his spine as he twisted to pinpoint her location. He spotted Skinner crouched low near one of doors leading out of the ballroom, but Nell wasn't with him. A second later the sheriff reached up to douse the lights.

"I'll cover the terrace doors." Daryl called to him from behind another plant. "Go find Nell."

Crawling on his belly, he moved quickly to the spot where he'd last seen her. The wood beneath his palms was still warm from her body. Fear pumped through his veins like a flooding river. His cell phone rang.

Not a number he recognized.

"Yes," he said.

"Keep everyone in the ballroom and tell Skinner to call off his volunteers. My partner will shoot to kill the next time. Nell has ten minutes to give me the necklace."

James Orbison. Reid barely recognized the voice because of the tone. Gone was the eager young scholar and journalist he'd questioned on the kitchen terrace earlier.

If he'd only acted sooner—he'd had all the evidence he needed seconds ago, when Cam had given him the description of two people who'd visited the Campbell estate seven months ago. And Edie had told him minutes before that Orbison had lied about coming to Edie's diner alone. According to Edie, he'd been with an older woman who'd acted besotted with him. She'd matched Gwen's description.

Ruthlessly, he shoved aside the recriminations. "Let me talk to Nell."

A beat went by, then Nell said, "I'm fine. I'm going to take James to where Eleanor hid the necklace."

An icy blade of fear sliced through Reid right to the

bone. The excitement in her voice told him that she'd figured out Eleanor's hiding place. But once she handed the necklace over, Orbison would kill her. Reid's only hope was to get to her first. Praying that the lack of light in the ballroom would cover his movements, Reid belly crawled his way back to Daryl and filled him in on his plan.

NELL STOPPED SHORT just as she and James passed the staircase in the foyer.

"Keep going." He jabbed the gun he was carrying into her back. "Giving me the necklace is the only way you're going to save the people you love. My partner will shoot someone the second I tell her to. Do you want a demonstration?"

His tone had Nell whirling to meet his eyes. There was a hardness and a steely determination that contrasted sharply with the one that her sister Adair and her aunt had described to her. Stiffening her knees to hide the shaking, she said, "The necklace isn't in the gazebo."

He grabbed her arm. "Don't toy with me. I know it's there."

Nell swallowed to ease the dryness in her throat. She was taking a huge gamble. Reid would come after her. Would he figure she was stalling and go to the gazebo? She had to bank on the fact that his instincts would guide him. "I discovered the listening device, and I said that to throw you off."

His eyes narrowed as his fingers bit into her arm. "If you're lying, all I have to do is press a button on my cell and someone inside the ballroom will die— starting with Reid Sutherland."

Nell pushed past the panic. "I'm not lying. Let me show you."

After a beat, he gestured with the gun. "Eight minutes—that's all you have left."

Past James's shoulder, she could see Eleanor's painting. She was acting on instinct and a guess, and everything depended on her being right. Taking a deep breath, she said, "Eleanor hid the necklace in her bedroom. There's a secret cupboard that Angus built for her."

"A secret cupboard."

Nell could almost see the wheels turning in his head.

"That would make sense," he said, a thread of excitement in his tone. "During those months when I was doing nightly research in your library, I looked for a second cupboard in that fireplace. Angus was the kind of man who would want the woman he loved to have one of her own. Then to make sure it remains a secret, he makes his own public knowledge and keeps all the attention on that. Distraction. Magicians use that same technique. Clever."

Nell climbed the stairs as slowly as she could. All she had was a theory. She had to keep him talking. "How do you know so much about Angus?"

"Research." He pushed her toward the stairs. "Eleanor Campbell kept diaries. I discovered them when I visited the Campbell estate in Scotland. She wrote about everything, including the story of the sapphires and how they came into the possession of Alistair MacGregor."

Nell stopped and looked over her shoulder at him. "Who is Alistair MacGregor?"

James jabbed the gun into her back. "Six minutes."

His cell phone rang.

"Have you got it?" The voice was faint but Nell could hear it.

"Not yet. She has six minutes left to give it to me. Let's give her an added incentive. Fire another bullet into the ballroom."

Nell stumbled at the sound of the shot. She had to buy more time. James Orbison wasn't a big man, but she doubted she could get the gun away from him. She'd already given him a hint of where to look for the necklace. The moment she led him into the bedroom, he might risk killing her and going after the sapphire necklace on her own.

"Five and a half minutes."

Get his mind off the clock. Keep him talking. "Who is Alistair MacGregor?"

"He was my great-great-great-great-grandfather's cousin, several times removed. I grew up hearing stories of how Mary Stuart gave her sapphires to his father in payment for saving her life, and how they mysteriously disappeared after Alistair's death. I've spent my life studying Mary Stuart and trying to find some trace of them. They belong to me."

"How did Eleanor get them?" Even as she asked the question, Nell thought of her dream and believed she already knew.

"Alistair fell so hard for Eleanor that he gave them to her as a betrothal gift. And she betrayed him." Hate and anger were clear in his voice. "Your beloved ancestor had no right to take them and run off with another man. They were never heard from again. There was no contact with the family as far as I could discover. Alistair hanged himself when he discovered what she'd done. That part wasn't in her diaries. She never knew she had caused that man's death. I found out from descendants of the servants." As they reached the door of the bedroom, he jabbed her with the gun. "I want what's mine."

Closing her hand around the doorknob, Nell swallowed hard. "You burned the library at the Campbell estate. Why?"

"To destroy any record legitimate heirs might use to claim the sapphires. They belong to me. Only me. She's appeared to me in dreams and told me that she wants me to have them."

Nell ignored the chill that flooded her. He was crazy. Obsession could do that to a person. Reminding herself to breathe, Nell opened the door to Eleanor's bedroom and crossed to the fireplace. He was right behind her, the gun in her back. *Stall.* "How in the world did you ever get mixed up with Gwendolen?"

"I came across her in my research. She's a true descendant of the Campbells. My plan was to use her and her stepdaughter and then let them take the fall when I disappeared with the sapphires. She also fancies herself in love with me, and she'll do anything I ask."

Or at least that's what she's made you believe. "Who's idea was it to run down my sister?"

"My suggestion. But Gwen was very agreeable. She blames your sister for putting her stepdaughter into a coma. I blame your sister for distracting Gwen. She's been less efficient since her stepdaughter went into the hospital. She was supposed to kill your boyfriend last night. But she intends to rectify her failure today. I wouldn't be surprised if she took him out with her first shot."

No. Nell had to exert all her self-control to prevent herself from shouting the word out loud. Not Reid.

Please not Reid. She would know if Gwen had succeeded in killing him because part of her would die, too.

   "Three minutes."

15

IN HIS MIND, Reid could hear a clock ticking as seconds sped away. He'd left taking out the shooter in Daryl's and Skinner's capable hands, but it had still taken precious minutes to get out of the ballroom. No time for second-guessing now. Not that he needed to. The Nell who he was coming to know would take Orbison straight to Eleanor and Angus's bedroom. Hitting the foyer at a dead run, he took the stairs three at a time.

Stall, Nell. Stall.

The words became a chant in his head as he reached the third floor and pushed through the double doors. Then he slowed his pace. He couldn't afford to alert Orbison. At the inner door, he paused. It was open a crack, which was large enough to reveal Nell kneeling at the left side of the fireplace. Orbison stood less than an arm's length away, his gun pointed at her back. Ruthlessly, he pushed feelings aside. A cool head was what he needed now. Slowly, he drew his weapon, aimed it and weighed the risks. If he took the shot, there was a chance Orbison's gun would go off. If he walked in, Orbison could grab Nell and use her as a shield.

If she found the necklace, Orbison would be distracted. That would be his moment to act. But that was a big *if.*

A trickle of sweat ran down his back as the ticking clock in his head grew louder. Nell traced her fingers along the stones of the fireplace. Not the side that opened Eleanor's cupboard. It was the side like the one used when Angus had built his secret cupboard in the main parlor. Of course. He'd built another one in this room so that Eleanor could hide her necklace in it. And Nell was going to find the priceless sapphires. When she did, he had to be ready.

"Two minutes," Orbison said.

Nell felt the jab of a gun in her back and fought against panic. She'd run her fingers over the rows of stones twice now, trying to find something that would open the cupboard. Had she been wrong?

Orbison jabbed her with the gun again. "Stop stalling."

"I'm not." Pushing against panic, she summoned up the image of the sketch that she was certain held the key to finding the necklace. Eleanor had drawn the fireplace at an angle that highlighted the left side. She ran her fingers over the first row of stones again. "It has to be here."

"Has to? You haven't seen the necklace?"

His voice had risen in pitch, and Nell swallowed hard against fear. "You said yourself that it makes sense that Angus would build a secret cupboard for Eleanor, then publicize his own to protect its existence. A classic case of distraction. I just need another minute."

"Thirty seconds."

As she began to search the third row, she caught a flicker of movement out of the corner of her eye. Reid. He was outside the door.

Fear stabbed sharper than ever. She had to buy time. "You said you researched the story of the sapphires and Alistair MacGregor. What did you find?"

"I found out who has the strongest claim on the sapphires, and it isn't you and your sisters or even Gwen. Although I convinced Gwen that her claim was stronger."

"Why is that?" Saying a little prayer, Nell continued along the third row.

"She is a descendent of Eleanor's oldest sister. I found proof of that. And Eleanor ran off with the jewels. Had she stayed in Scotland after Alistair MacGregor's death, the sapphires would have belonged to the family. So in a sense she stole them. It would have made a strong legal argument, but once we found out that someone had a stronger claim, I convinced Gwen that a much better plan would be to simply take them."

Nell feathered her fingers down to the final row of stones. "Who has a stronger claim?"

"Are you just playing dumb? Or are you simply stalling because you think someone is coming to rescue you?"

"No." Her heart jumped when she felt the tiny depression in the stones. But she needed a minute. "What are you talking about? Who has a stronger legal claim than Eleanor's descendants?"

"Alistair MacGregor's true heirs. After his death, his estate went to a cousin twice removed, Ennis Sutherland. Your friends, Reid, Duncan and Cam, are the only remaining Sutherlands left in that line. But the jewels belong to me. And your thirty seconds are up."

The gun stabbed sharply into her back. Even as panic threatened, she felt the tiny gap between the stones. Easing her fingertips into it, she pulled. A foot square section of the fireplace swung silently open. When she saw the suede pouch lying inside, her heart skipped a beat. Fingers shaking, she opened the flap and slipped out the necklace. The jewels caught every bit of the light in the room, gleaming as blue as the surface of the lake at its deepest point. They grew warm in her hands, and for a second she was sure she felt the presence of the woman who'd so carefully hidden them away. And she felt the love.

"Mine."

The rasp in Orbison's voice brought reality back with a snap. Reid. He hadn't made a move yet because of her. And when he did, Nell didn't doubt that James Orbison would shoot him. She had to distract Orbison. Clasping the necklace tightly in her left hand, she held it to her side out of his sight as she rose and turned.

"Let me see it."

Slowly, she raised her hand, the jewels dripping from her fingers. Orbison's gaze dropped to the sapphires—just as she'd hoped.

"Lovely," he murmured. "They're more beautiful than I imagined. You can carry the memory of them into the next world."

Out of the corner of her eye, she saw the door swing open and a figure step into the room. But Orbison caught the movement, also. The hand that was reaching for the jewels was suddenly around her neck and the muzzle of Orbison's gun pressed hard into her temple.

"How nice of you to join us, Mr. Sutherland. It will be better for Nell if you put the gun down right now."

Don't. Nell tried to get the word out, but the arm around her neck cut off her breath.

Reid let one full beat go by before he let the gun drop. Then he raised his hands, palms outward. "Let her go."

Orbison laughed. "After all the trouble she's caused?"

"She found the necklace."

"Good point. I'll make her death as quick and painless as possible."

"You won't get away with it," Reid said, his voice calm. "You'll never make it off the castle grounds. And you haven't killed anyone yet."

"High time I did then." Orbison took the gun from her temple and swung it toward Reid.

The instant his grip on her loosened, Nell used all her weight and the adrenaline of terror to stomp hard on James Orbison's foot. Twisting, she grabbed the arm that held the weapon with both hands. The sound of the shot deafened her as she used all her weight to shove him to the floor.

She was barely aware of pain and the coppery flavor of fear in her mouth as she scrambled to straddle him, never losing her grip on the wrist that held the gun. "You are not going to shoot Reid. He's mine."

They rolled once, twice. Nell used all her strength to hold on. But her hands had become slippery, and Orbison was strong. She couldn't keep him from raising the gun again. In seconds, he would have it pointed at her.

Reid stood frozen. He'd retrieved his gun, but he couldn't get a clear shot. Then everything happened so quickly that immediately afterward he wasn't sure of the sequence. Nell still had the sapphire necklace wrapped around one of her wrists, and suddenly it caught all the light in the room and nearly blinded him.

It did blind Orbison. Fully.

"Mine." The greedy voice was almost drowned out by the clatter of his gun hitting the floor when Nell knocked it out of his hand. He reached for the necklace. As Reid moved for him, he saw Nell smash her fist into Orbison's face. Reid kicked the gun aside and pulled Nell off. He made quick work of using Orbison's belt to secure his hands.

Pushing her hair out of her face, Nell watched Reid work quickly, efficiently. She felt as if she were watching a movie. It was over. And Reid was alive. Relief. That's why she felt dizzy. And her arm was stinging. Glancing down, she saw the red stain on her shirt. "Reid…"

He turned to face her. "I had it under control. You could have been shot."

"I think I was shot." She might have laughed if it hadn't been for the second wave of dizziness. Then all she felt was Reid's arms around her as the world went black.

With fear snaking through his gut, Reid pulled Nell into his arms and cradled her on his lap. Feeling the warmth of her blood on his hands, he had to swallow hard. He should have protected her from this, and he hadn't. Not that she'd needed him. She'd fought Orbison like a demon.

Ignoring the thoughts of blame, he ripped off the sleeve of her shirt and made himself examine the wound. The bullet had gone cleanly through the flesh. Nell's flesh. His stomach rolled.

It was only slightly deeper than a scratch, he told himself as he used her shirt to bandage it tightly. By the time he finished, his throat was dry from the rawness of his breathing. He heard footsteps pounding in the corridor outside. While he waited for the cavalry, he held her close, rocking her. "You're going to be fine. You're going to be fine."

"Yes," she murmured without opening her eyes. "He wanted to kill you. I couldn't…let him do that. Because I love you, and I never kissed you beneath the stones."

Reid felt his heart take a long tumble. He opened his mouth to say something, but before he could even form a word, Daryl burst into the room.

"She took him out, but not before he shot her," Reid said. "A flesh wound. She's going to be fine." If he said it often enough, he'd start to believe it. "We need a doctor."

"Glad you left something for me to do," Daryl said as he punched a number into his cell phone. "Our Gwen is neutralized thanks to Skinner. That man has good moves. If he were twenty years younger, I'd recruit him."

Reid paced back and forth outside the door to Nell's bedroom. A headache pulsed at his temple as thoughts and fears danced through his mind. When he'd lain her on the bed, she'd looked so small, so pale, she might have been dead. The moment the doctor from the clinic at nearby Huntleigh College had arrived, she'd cleared the room of everyone but Vi. That had been nearly half an hour ago.

"Nell is going to be fine." Daryl pocketed his cell phone and leaned against the wall. "Our local doctor is very good. The college hired her when she retired from the E.R. at Boston General. Her record there was stellar. I checked her out."

Reid ran his hands through his hair. "We didn't check deeply enough into Orbison."

"I agree that we didn't do it quickly enough. But the reports that I've had in the past half hour from Cam and my man in D.C. substantiated everything he told you. Your maternal grandfather is a direct descendant of Ennis Sutherland, so you and your brothers have a legitimate claim on those sapphires."

Reid waved a dismissive hand as he continued to pace. "Do you think I care about that?"

Daryl chuckled. "Not yet. But it was the main motivation behind everything Orbison did. Obsessed as he was with getting his hands on the sapphires, he did everything he could to destroy any evidence of that claim."

As Daryl answered a call on his cell, Reid's mind veered once more to what Nell had told him just before she'd lost consciousness. She loved him. The emotions those words had triggered were still spinning through his system. He also recalled what she'd told Orbison in those seconds when Reid had stood helpless and watched her struggle with Orbison. "He's mine." But she'd spoken in the heat of the moment. She might not even remember.

"That was Skinner," Daryl said as he pocketed his phone. "Gwen is furious with Orbison, and she's singing like a bird. The only thing more dangerous than a woman scorned is a con woman who's been outconned."

The doctor stepped out of Nell's bedroom. When Reid made a move to go in, she placed a firm hand on his chest. "She's a lucky girl. She's going to be fine, but she needs her rest. I cleaned and bandaged the wound and left her a sedative."

"I have to see her," Reid said.

The doctor stood her ground. "She won't take that sedative if you go in there. Whatever it is, it can wait until morning."

No. It can't. Reid barely kept himself from shouting the words.

"I'll make some tea," Vi said, drawing the doctor down the hall. Reluctantly, Reid followed to the head of the stairs. Then he paused, waiting until the two women rounded the landing and began their descent to the foyer. "I have to call Cam," he said to Daryl.

"I'll tell the doc that you'll join us shortly." Smiling, he patted Reid's shoulder before Cam ambled after the two women. At the landing, he paused. "If you're smart, you'll take her out to the stone arch. That's where I would have taken Vi if she hadn't beat me to it."

The stones. Daryl was right. Whirling, he strode back to Nell's room. The only way to settle things between them was to talk beneath Angus's arch. He was reaching for the knob when the door swung open.

"We have to talk." They spoke the words together. When Nell grabbed his shirt to pull him into the room, he swept her up and into his arms.

"Where—"

"We're going to finish this once and for all under Angus and Eleanor's stones."

Finish? A band of pain tightened around Nell's heart, and it sharpened with each step Reid took. He was down the stairs in seconds. Tapping in the security code delayed him only a few more, and then he was running with her through the gardens.

He wanted to finish things between them.

Nell drew in a breath and felt the burn in her lungs. Night sounds filled the air—the hoot of an owl, the soft rush of wind through the trees, and farther away, the lapping of the water against the shore. She had to think. If he wanted to end things between them and walk away, doing it beneath the stone arch made some sense. To her knowledge, no one had ever used the stones that way before. But if kissing beneath the stones bound you to a person for life, breaking up beneath the arch might also tap into the power of the legend.

She could imagine Reid developing a strategy like that. She could even see herself writing it that way. In fact, for her book, it would make a great opening scene. Her hero and heroine who'd kissed beneath the stones would break up there, trying to undo the spell. It would definitely add a layer of conflict to the plot, and it would serve as a trigger to the romance. And Alistair MacGregor's tragic love story would serve as a background to everything. It would add a layer of tragedy to her book.

A mix of panic and fear bubbled up when he stepped into the wide arc of light that surrounded the stone arch. This was *her* story. And it was not going to end the way Alistair's had. Nor was she going to allow Reid to break up with her. She was going to use the power of the legend before he could.

The instant Reid stepped beneath the stones, she grabbed his face, drew his lips to hers and planted a kiss. She'd meant it as a statement, but the moment his mouth covered hers, her intention changed. Everything else faded but Reid, and she let herself simply sink into him—his scent, his taste, the strength of his arms wrapped so tightly around her. This was what she wanted. This was everything she wanted. She was never going to let him go.

When he finally drew back, she had to tell herself to breathe, to swallow, to think. She was stunned, when he dropped his hands to his side, to discover she remained upright.

"Nell…"

Shadows prevented her from reading his eyes. But his action had been clear. How could he have kissed her like that and still want to finish things between them?

"Nell," he repeated. "I brought you out here to talk."

A flare of anger stiffened her spine, and she jabbed a finger into his chest. "Save your breath. No amount of talking is going to change what's between us. I kissed you, and you kissed me back. It's settled."

"Nell…"

She poked him again, hard enough to send him back a step. "You're going to say you didn't want this. Too bad." Whirling, she paced to the side of the arch and then turned back, her chin lifted. "Neither did I. But a girl has a right to change her mind. And now it's too late. We're stuck with each other. End of story."

Reid walked toward her then. It wasn't what he had planned, but then nothing had been from the day he'd encountered her again. "Okay." When he took her hand and linked their fingers, the surprise in her eyes gave him some satisfaction.

"You're not going to argue?"

Raising their joined hands, he kissed her fingers. "You kissed me under the stones. I love you, Nell MacPherson. We are definitely stuck with each other."

She gripped his fingers hard as if she were determined to never let him go. "Then why did you stop kissing me?"

"Because in another moment, I was going to do more than that." He lifted her in his arms. "You've been shot. I have to get you back to the castle."

"Wait." Her grip on him tightened.

"Nell…"

Her smile had his determination wavering. "I'll go quietly on two conditions. First, I get a rain check on the kiss and 'more than that,' and second, we just sit here on the ledge for a minute."

Reid sat and settled her on his lap. When she snuggled her head into the crook of his shoulder, nothing had ever felt so right.

"I love you, too," she said.

His laugh blended with the whisper of the wind in the trees and the far-off sound of the water. "I got the message when you kissed me." He tipped her chin up. "I brought you out here to talk you into marrying me and beginning a new life together. Thank God you are a woman of action."

"That's just what Angus must have done with Eleanor."

Reid glanced out over the gardens to the castle and the lake. "I can almost feel them here."

"Can you? I thought the practical Secret Service agent didn't believe in that kind of woo-woo."

"It gets better. Remember that theory you had that Angus helped her hide the jewels so that you and your sisters would find them? I'm willing to buy into that, too. It's the only scenario I can come up with to explain how they ended up back where Eleanor would have wanted them—with Alistair MacGregor's heirs.

I don't know how he did it, but Angus found a way to help her deal with the guilt she felt."

"It makes sense. When you consider that Angus spent his entire life granting Eleanor's every wish, it's a logical conclusion. I am sure I can use it in the book I am writing. I'm going to weave in all the aspects of Angus and Eleanor's story—even the tragedy of Alistair's death." She reached up to place her palms on his cheeks and looked into his eyes. "And, of course, the hero and heroine, after fighting against it for the length of the story, will find their happy ending, as we finally have."

"No." Reid brushed his lips softly over hers. "Not an ending. This is just the beginning of our story."

Then he kissed her again beneath the stones.

* * * * *

#775 COWBOYS & ANGELS
Sons of Chance
by Vicki Lewis Thompson

The last person ranch hand Trey Wheeler expects to meet at a ski lodge is the woman who saved him from a car crash. Elle Masterson is way more tempting than your average guardian angel—and Trey wants to be tempted....

#776 A SOLDIER'S CHRISTMAS
Uniformly Hot!
by Leslie Kelly, Joanne Rock and Karen Foley

When they come home for Christmas, three military heroes have visions in their heads of things far sexier than sugarplums. But the women they love want more than just one very good night....

#777 THE MIGHTY QUINNS: DEX
The Mighty Quinns
by Kate Hoffmann

When Irish news cameraman Dex Kennedy takes on a documentary project, he doesn't realize that the job will uncover some startling family secrets—and put him in the path of a sexy American producer who is all business. Except in the bedroom!

#778 NAUGHTY CHRISTMAS NIGHTS
by Tawny Weber

Romance vs sex? Designer Hailey North is determined her lacy lingerie will be the new holiday line at Rudolph's Department Stores. Gage Milano is providing competition with his hot leather look. But in the nights leading up to Christmas, things are heating up—between Hailey and Gage!

YOU CAN FIND MORE INFORMATION ON UPCOMING HARLEQUIN® TITLES, FREE EXCERPTS AND MORE AT WWW.HARLEQUIN.COM.

REQUEST YOUR FREE BOOKS!
2 FREE NOVELS PLUS 2 FREE GIFTS!

red-hot reads!

YES! Please send me 2 FREE Harlequin® Blaze™ novels and my 2 FREE gifts (gifts are worth about $10). After receiving them, if I don't wish to receive any more books, I can return the shipping statement marked "cancel." If I don't cancel, I will receive 4 brand-new novels every month and be billed just $4.74 per book in the U.S. or $4.96 per book in Canada. That's a savings of at least 14% off the cover price. It's quite a bargain. Shipping and handling is just 50¢ per book in the U.S. and 75¢ per book in Canada.* I understand that accepting the 2 free books and gifts places me under no obligation to buy anything. I can always return a shipment and cancel at any time. Even if I never buy another book, the two free books and gifts are mine to keep forever.

150/350 HDN F4WC

Name _____ (PLEASE PRINT) _____

Address _____ Apt. # _____

City _____ State/Prov. _____ Zip/Postal Code _____

Signature (if under 18, a parent or guardian must sign) _____

Mail to the Harlequin® Reader Service:
IN U.S.A.: P.O. Box 1867, Buffalo, NY 14240-1867
IN CANADA: P.O. Box 609, Fort Erie, Ontario L2A 5X3

Want to try two free books from another line?
Call 1-800-873-8635 or visit www.ReaderService.com.

* Terms and prices subject to change without notice. Prices do not include applicable taxes. Sales tax applicable in N.Y. Canadian residents will be charged applicable taxes. Offer not valid in Quebec. This offer is limited to one order per household. Not valid for current subscribers to Harlequin Blaze books. All orders subject to credit approval. Credit or debit balances in a customer's account(s) may be offset by any other outstanding balance owed by or to the customer. Please allow 4 to 6 weeks for delivery. Offer available while quantities last.

Your Privacy—The Harlequin® Reader Service is committed to protecting your privacy. Our Privacy Policy is available online at www.ReaderService.com or upon request from the Harlequin Reader Service.

We make a portion of our mailing list available to reputable third parties that offer products we believe may interest you. If you prefer that we not exchange your name with third parties, or if you wish to clarify or modify your communication preferences, please visit us at www.ReaderService.com/consumerchoice or write to us at Harlequin Reader Service Preference Service, P.O. Box 9062, Buffalo, NY 14269. Include your complete name and address.

HBI3R2

"We can't kiss again. We have to keep things strictly professional from here on out."

"Of course," Dex said. "I completely agree. And I can do that." He grabbed Marlie's hand and pulled her back down next to him.

They stared at each other for a long moment. "You're thinking about kissing me again, aren't you?" She sighed softly. "Maybe we just ought to do it again so we can move on."

Dex nodded. "You're right, it probably would help."

She drew a deep breath and forced a smile. "So, I guess you should just do it and get it over with."

"Right," Dex murmured.

Hell, he knew if he kissed her again, the attraction would never go away. It would just get worse. And then having to pretend that it didn't exist while they worked together would be pure torture. But he wasn't about to refuse her invitation He wasn't a bloody eedjit.

Dex slipped his hand around her nape, his fingers tangling in her hair. He gently drew her close and touched his lips to hers. But the moment they made contact, he knew he was lost. A need so fierce, so overwhelming, surged up inside of him. He wanted to touch her, to kiss her, to tear her clothes off and make love to her until his body was exhausted and his mind was quiet.

Dex took a chance and pulled her even closer, his tongue teasing at her lips, searching for the warmth of her mouth and her unspoken surrender. When she opened beneath the assault, he groaned softly and drew her body on top of his, lying back on the sofa.

He needed this, a chance to clear his head of all the dark memories, all the twisted guilt that plagued his every waking minute. If he could just find some peace, if only for one night, maybe he could put his life back on track.

As their kiss grew more intense, Dex pulled her beneath him, desperate to feel her body against his. He stared down at her, his fingers brushing strands of hair from her face. Her lashes fluttered and the color was high in her cheeks. God, she was so beautiful, so perfect. The prospect of losing himself in her warmth was too tempting to deny.

She opened her eyes, their gazes meeting, and for a moment, he thought she was going to speak.

"What?" he murmured.

"I—I think that's enough," Marlie murmured.

"No," he whispered. "It's not nearly enough."

**Pick up THE MIGHTY QUINNS: DEX
by Kate Hoffmann, available November 19,
wherever you buy Harlequin® Blaze® books.**